Devilish King

Valentino Empire, Book 1

Kylie Kent

Ebook ISBN:9780645257243
Paperback ISBN: 978-0-6452572-8-1

Cover illustration by
Stacy Garcia - Graphics By Stacy

Editing services provided by
Kat Pagan – https://www.facebook.com/PaganProofreading

Dedication

To Mel, thank you for being that friend. The one who understands my version of crazy like no other. The one who embraces my crazy four a.m. thoughts and talks me off the cliff when I want to kill off all the main characters. Thank you for being that one friend who will follow me down dark alleys, in hopes of getting kidnapped and finding our future mafia boss husbands.

Prologue

Holly

"I can't believe you're doing this, Rye. It's insane. Are you sure you don't want to wait just a little longer?" I know my question is falling on love-deafened ears. My twin sister, Reilly, the one who swore black and blue she would never fall into the marriage trap, that she'd never trust a man with her heart... Well, she's eating those words now, as we currently stand inside a dressing room in Vegas.

Yes, Vegas... Bray, her husband-to-be, flew us all to Vegas because, in his own words: *I'm not waiting another goddamn day to make Reilly my wife.* As far as brothers-in-law go, I don't hate the thought of Bray being mine. He's great; it's clear just how much he loves my sister. Fiercely. I don't really have any objections to the union, but I do feel it's my sisterly duty to let her know it's okay to change her mind at the last minute.

"I'm more than sure, Hol. I can't imagine *not* spending the rest of my life with him." Her smile lights up her face. "Plus, there's also that damn pierced cucumber. I just can't give that thing up. It's an addiction like no other."

"Ew, gross." This response comes from Ella, Bray's eighteen-year-old sister.

"You know, I have to agree with Ella. *Ew, gross*—and let's not ever mention Bray's cucumber again." Alyssa scrunches up her face; she's one of our best friends and also happens to be newly married to Bray's brother, Zac. "Come on, El, let's go clean out our innocent ears."

Alyssa shuts the door behind them, leaving me alone with Reilly. I feel like I haven't really had much one-on-one time with my sister since... well, since she met Bray. Their start was rough; it took Reilly a while to come to terms with the idea of being in love. Then, when she had finally accepted it, Bray got shot and ended up in a coma. Those were a hard few months,

2

watching Reilly try to be strong, when she was actually breaking down inside.

I still blame myself for Bray's injury. If I hadn't walked into that building... *at that moment*... If the gun hadn't turned on me... If I had done *something*, instead of nothing—instead of freezing—would he have been so stupid? Would he have antagonized that madman? I can't even remember what Bray said, but he managed to get the barrel trained back on him within seconds. *Seconds*... I only had that gun pointed at me for seconds—yet those same, few, frozen seconds changed everything.

Shaking the thoughts from my head, I focus back on the here and now. It's Reilly's wedding day. I won't let anything ruin this.

"You know, I'd always envisioned Dad walking me down the aisle..." My twin looks out the window.

"Obviously, he would be here if he could, Rye. It's probably breaking his heart, knowing this is happening without him." The feelings I have for my father are hard to even acknowledge. I love him—*he's my dad*. He was the one man I could always depend on when we were growing up.

Until life went to shit...

First, my brother was killed by a drunk driver. Then, my dad took matters into his own hands after that driver got off with little more than a slap on the wrist. On the day of the court hearing, I learnt how my dad had shot the guy point blank. *In the head.* And our family hasn't been the same since. Mum, Reilly, and I have stuck together, doing our best to support each other through all of this.

"I know, but I just... It'd just be nice if they could be here: Mum, Dad... Dylan." Reilly gets a distant look in her eyes before shaking her head. "At least I have you. We'll always have each other, Hol. That's enough for me."

Crap... As soon as Bray woke up from his coma, I decided I wasn't satisfied going through the motions of everyday life anymore. I decided to make a change. I want to live. I want to experience things I never would have dreamt of before.

That's why I applied for a working visa and a teaching job in New York. And to my surprise, I got both. I haven't told Reilly yet, but I won't be travelling back to Sydney with them next week. I'll be heading straight from here to The Big Apple. Straight to my new life. My new adventures. The new Holly.

Chapter One

Holly

*O*kay, Holly, you've got this. Just one foot in front of the other. You can do it.

I can do it. I'm a grown-ass woman for God's sake. How hard can it be to navigate my way through the JFK Airport? Extremely freaking hard, considering I've always managed to get lost in Sydney, which seems like nothing but a tiny airstrip in comparison to what I'm looking at now.

I count down from ten—to try to relax my frayed nerves. I only manage to get to eight before someone shoves into me without so much as a glance or apology. I'm not even out of the airport, and I'm already questioning my decision (and my sanity) in choosing New York as the place to find the new me.

Holly 2.0? Yeah, she's nowhere to be seen yet. My eyes are starting to sting. I clamp my hands into fists at my sides. I will not cry—well, not here anyway. I'll wait until I'm behind closed doors, where no one can see me. *Or my meltdown.* Thanks to the trust fund my dad set up for me, I was able to score an awesome-looking apartment in Carnegie Hill.

I've refused to touch that money for the last five years. Mostly because I was pissed off at my dad—*still am*. But desperate times and all... There's not exactly a lot you can get on a teacher's salary in New York. I didn't want to be making a long commute to work every day, so I tapped into that account and paid a six-month lease on a cute little one-bedroom, one-bathroom unit.

The school I'll be teaching at is elite. According to their website, it's super selective and high tech, with a bloody ten-year waiting list. *Though I'm not entirely sure who the hell is enrolling a child before they are even born yet.* The facilities are state of the art—*no expense spared*, or so I'm told—while the faculty is made up of the best and the brightest in their fields.

Despite a little culture shock, I'm actually excited to settle into my new classroom.

That being said, I have two weeks to *settle* into this new city first. And somehow, I feel like *that* is going to be harder than I first thought. Determination has me straightening my spine, picking my head up, and following the crowd to baggage claim. I can do this. My phone clenched in one hand, my other clutching the strap of my carry-on bag on my shoulder, I stalk forward.

Everything is going to be okay.

Twenty minutes later, I'm finally sitting in a cab on my way to my new apartment. Butterflies fill my stomach as both nerves and excitement flutter about. The landlord said he'd be there when I arrived to hand over the keys and show me inside. I still have to finish furnishing the apartment. I was able to organize a bedroom suite and linen, scheduling to have them delivered a few days ago—the landlord was kind enough to send me a photo of the layout. I'll arrange everything else over the next two weeks. I'm looking forward to it, actually. Putting my own touches on my own space. Did I mention this is the first time I've ever lived by myself?

Up until now, I've lived with my mother. And until Reilly met Bray, so did she. I wonder how Mum is doing by herself now... I'm sure she'll be fine. She's the strongest person I know. She's already endured the worst thing that could ever happen to someone: losing a child. And not long after, she lost her husband as well, though he *is* still alive and she could go visit him. If he'd let her...

My dad has a thing about not wanting my mum to see him behind bars, so they haven't been face-to-face since that day in court. Instead, they write letters to each other every week. How their love has stayed intact through everything, I have no idea. But I envy it. I want it. One day. Not today though. Today, I am happy to explore and navigate this new life. *By myself.*

No expectations. No real major life goals or plans, other than just *to be.*

"This is it, ma'am." The taxi driver stops by a block of tall townhouses and cranes his neck to look at me. "That'll be fifty-six."

"Okay, thank you." I withdraw the cash from my wallet. I know I'm supposed to tip him... I just don't know how much. And I don't want to be rude either, so I grab another ten before handing over the money.

"I'll get your bags for you."

"Thanks." Stepping out onto the sidewalk, I look up.

So, this is it... The area is nice, not overly busy, with just a few people walking the tree-lined streets. The driver approaches with my suitcase. I glance towards the stairs, trying to figure out how I'm going to navigate my way up those ten steps. And before I can even consider looking to the driver for help, he jumps back in the car and speeds off, leaving me standing on the sidewalk still staring up at the brick building that is now my home. *Right, no time like the present.* I grab the handle of my suitcase and struggle to lift it onto the first step. Nine to go.

It takes about ten minutes, but I've finally managed to get to the landing, although my suitcase looks like it's seen better days. I find the button for apartment five and press it. I don't have to wait long before a male voice comes across the speaker.

"Hello."

"Ah, hi. It's Holly." What am I meant to say? *Let me in?*

"Hi, babe, just push on the door when you hear the buzzer. Hit the elevator for the second floor," he says, his tone as bored as batshit.

Babe? Really? I feel the urge to correct him. *My name is Holly, not babe.* But I don't. Instead, I shuffle my way inside, thanking the gods there's a lift in sight— and that I don't have to navigate up another set of stairs.

What I'm not prepared for is to have someone waiting right there, as the lift opens to the second floor. I take a step back before straightening my spine and marching out of the confined space.

"Holly, I'm Greg, your new landlord. Nice to meet you." The guy standing in front of me is wearing a well-fitted suit. Okay, so maybe my first impression (you know, that this guy's a total douchebag) was a little off. I hold out my free hand to shake his.

"Hi, thanks for showing me around. It's great to meet you too." I smile politely and try my best not to recoil when he brings my hand to his lips and kisses it before letting go.

"My pleasure. Boy, that accent. You are going to be a hot little commodity around here." He smirks, looking me up and down.

And just like that, I retract my prior statement: this guy *is* a douchebag... of epic proportions.

"I don't want to seem rude or anything, but I'm a little jet-lagged. And honestly, buggered. I just want to get settled in and sleep for the next week."

"Right, of course. Sorry... follow me."

My stomach twists at the thought of being alone with him in that apartment. I don't really have a choice though. My mind goes back over all the self-defense steps Bray insisted on teaching me when he discovered my future plans.

I watch as Greg disengages the deadbolt on the door, grateful there is a decent-looking lock on the place. He steps over the threshold and holds the door open for me. I have to squeeze past him to enter, but I manage to do it without brushing up against him. *Thankfully*.

He's a good-looking guy, in a boy-next-door kind of way. Sandy-blonde hair, blue eyes, and dimples. He has the appearance of that typical American male you see in movies. Yet, there is just something a little... *off*... about him. The way he's leering at me makes my skin prickle and the hair on the back of my neck stand on end—like the first victim in a horror film. The one everyone is screaming at to *hurry up and run.*

I need to get this over with (and get *this* man out of *this* apartment) as quickly as I can. Turning, I hold out my hand. "Thank you again... for meeting me here," I say, waiting for him to relinquish the keys he's holding.

He looks down at my open palm, then back up to my eyes. "Sure, no problem. Want me to give you the tour?" he asks, still clutching the cold metal in his fist.

I look behind me. It's a small open-plan living room. *Small is an understatement.* There's a tiny kitchenette, and I can see two doors down the narrow hallway from where I'm standing. I think I just had the tour. "Ah, no, it's fine. I'm pretty sure I've got it," I say, turning back to him, my open palm screaming the words I don't. *Hand 'em over and get out!*

"Right, here you go. Rent's due on the first of each month." He reluctantly surrenders the keys and pivots on his heel. I shut the door and lock it as soon as he's past the threshold. Leaning against the frame, I drop to the ground and let the tears—the ones I've been holding back since the airport—fall freely this time.

What the hell have I done? Why did I think I could do this? It doesn't matter how far I move, or how much I change my life, I'm always going to be the same old Holly. Quiet Holly, who blindly follows her twin sister around. Shy Holly, who would rather be sitting at home reading a book, than actually talking to people.

Scared Holly, who (ever since Bray's shooting) has been afraid of her own bloody shadow.

I swipe angrily at the tears. *I can do this.* I need to do this. Standing, I drag my suitcase down the hall before opening the first door I see: a small bathroom. I head for the next door, which is the bedroom. Kicking my shoes off, I flop down on the empty mattress. I'll get up soon and grab some linens.

Chapter Two

Holly

The incessant ringing breaks through my sleep-fogged brain. I reach out an arm, trying to swipe my phone off the bedside table, but end up with a handful of air. I bolt upright, scanning my surroundings. It's dark, with the only glow of light coming from the floor where my phone's illuminated screen is lying in wait.

The ringing stops before it starts back up again straight away. I breathe a sigh of relief once recognition settles in. It's okay. I'm in my own apartment. There's nothing to be afraid of here. I jump off the bed, pick up the phone, and realize it's two a.m. I must have been really jet-lagged. I never intended to actually sleep when I went to lie down.

"Reilly, it's two in the morning. Why are you calling me?" I answer.

"Well, thank God. Bray, it's okay. She's alive!" Reilly yells out, not bothering to move her mouth away from the phone and deafening me in the process.

"I'm alive. *Obviously.* I was asleep."

"I've been trying to call you for the last two hours, Holly. I had Bray booking flights to New York, so I could come and hunt down your murderer and avenge your death." I know she's joking. At least, I hope she is... I don't laugh though; the whole *avenging death* isn't a laughing matter in our family. That's exactly how my dad ended up behind bars. "Shit, sorry, Hol. I was kidding. Mostly," Reilly says. "So, how's The Big Apple? Huh, I just got it."

"Got what?" My brain is still too far in sleep land for her riddles.

"The Big Apple. You moving to a city called The Big Apple. It's ironic, because you're a teacher and teachers eat apples and all that."

"I haven't had nearly enough sleep or coffee to even summon up a response to that one, Rye."

"You should have called. I was worried. I don't do worried very well. I think I actually got a few gray hairs, which I'm sure if you look in the mirror, you'll have them too."

"Rye, you're a redhead. You'll be safe from gray hairs for a while yet."

"Well, I need you to call me—*every day*. Let's set a time, and if you don't check in at that time every day, then I'll book a flight to come hunt down your murderer."

"Or here's a thought. Let's not," I suggest. I have no intention of playing into her neurotic control freak of a mind.

"Okay, I'm thinking four p.m. New York time. Call me, text, send photo evidence—like the day's newspaper with your face in the picture, so I know it's you."

"Rye, I gotta go. I need to find food and coffee. I came straight from the airport and crashed. I'll call you later."

"Okay, but promise me you'll really call. Please, Holly." Reilly's tone is more serious; she's on the verge of tears. I can hear how hard this is for her. I have to get off the phone before I start crying, or spontaneously tell her that I'm coming home.

"I promise. I'm okay, Rye. And I promise I'll be careful, and I'll call you later."

"I just really love you, Holly, like as much as I love myself, and that's a freaking lot."

"I love you too, Rye. What's not to love? You're a carbon copy of me." I laugh.

"Okay, call me back later."

"I will." I hang up the phone and look around the eerily quiet room. I should make the bed—all the bedding is in a pile at the foot of it. I'll get to it after coffee. I pull my phone out and do a Google search to see if there's any place to get some caffeine and food, preferably nearby and open at two a.m.

I guess it's true what they say: *New York really is the city that never sleeps.* The list of restaurants, cafés, and bars within walking distance is endless. I throw on my coat, slip my feet back into my boots, and grab my purse. Locking up, I don't consider that it's literally the middle of the night, and I'm about to walk the streets of New York. *By myself.* Until my feet hit the pavement...

There are a few people brushing past. *I can do this.* The sidewalks are lit up with heaps of streetlights. Looking down at my phone, I see that I just need to walk a few blocks until I get to a business district. There's a twenty-four-hour café that came up on my search, so that's where I'm headed.

There's a slight chill in the air, but it's not too cold. It's just colder than how I'm used to September being. This is when it starts warming up in Sydney, easing you into the scorching summer months. But this year, I'll get that white Christmas I've always dreamed of having. I can't wait to see the snow, to experience a New York winter.

The song "Empire State of Mind" by Alicia Keys plays on repeat in my head as I walk down the street. This is where I'll discover the new me. I'm confident that exciting things are going to happen here. I'm going to love this city. I can blend into the crowd, get lost with the herd, and not be noticed.

I can be anything—and anyone—I want to be here. Nobody knows me. Nobody knows my family's history.

They don't know my brother died.

They don't know that my dad murdered his killer and ended up behind bars.

They don't know that I'm the twin sister of Reilly Williamson, who is the wife of Bray Williamson.

They don't know me.

With this knowledge, I hold my head high. I try to smile at people as I pass by, but I get weary looks in return as they step farther aside to give me a wider berth. Okay, note to self: *tone down the smiling.* I probably look like a crazy person.

After ten minutes, I find the twenty-four-hour café. I made it here in one piece. *See? I can do this.* Pushing on the heavy door, I'm engulfed by the warmth of the fire that's blazing off to the side. It feels homey, with big soft-looking brown leather couches surrounding the mantelpiece. Surprisingly, no one is sitting there, although the booths are plenty full of patrons.

It's odd that this many people are out at two a.m. on a Tuesday night. I look around, thinking I'll just find a booth, but those couches... that fire... They're calling to me. Smiling at the waitress, who happened to peek up as I entered the store, I walk over and drop into one of the single sofas next to the hearth.

And all the commotion suddenly stops. I glance over and everyone seems to be purposely looking away from me. Everyone except the waitress—she's now staring my way with wide eyes.

Great, just my luck. The first place I choose to visit in this city, and it must be getting robbed. My strangled breaths part my lips, my heart rate picks up, and my palms sweat. This can't be happening to me.

I arch my neck, needing to see what's going on. Except... nothing's happening. I don't see anyone holding out a gun. No one is yelling demands. People aren't scrambling to hide under tables. No, they're all just looking at me, or trying to inconspicuously look in my direction.

I peek down at my coat and wipe at my face. What the bloody hell are they all gawking at? I can feel the red creep up my neck. My hands shake a little as I fidget with my purse. I pull my phone out, deciding to focus on that. Maybe they'll all turn away once they realize I'm no one special.

I scroll through my Insta feed—but the more I scan the photos, the more homesick I feel. I hear the chime signaling someone's entrance. *Do not look up, Holly.*

I keep my eyes on my phone, like it's the most interesting thing I've ever seen. The hair on the back of my neck stands up and chills sweep over my body. This is more than just a room full of people staring at me. This reaction is different. I remind myself not to look up.

My eyes stay on my screen, even when I hear a gravelly voice say something loudly in what sounds like Italian. As much as I want to sneak a glance, to see who the owner of that voice is, I don't. I count to ten. My knee shakes as I fight my body's response to that voice. I get to five before I give in and raise my eyes. But all I see are the backs of two men walking through a door labeled: *staff only*.

Maybe they're the owners.

When I peer around the café again, I note that everyone has gone back to eating, drinking, and whatever else they were doing before they were staring at me like I'm the new circus freak in town. Even the waitress appears to have recovered from whatever *that* was. She strolls over to me with a huge smile on her face and a notepad in her hand. I notice a slight tremor to her fingers as she grips the pen tightly.

"Good evening, what can I get for you, ma'am?" she asks politely.

"Oh, hi! Um, I haven't had a chance to look at the menu. What's good?"

"Oh my, you're Australian?" Her smile is genuine now.

"I am," I answer, unsure what else to say to that.

"I've always wanted to go to Australia. It's on my bucket list."

"Oh, you should. It's a great country," I urge, picking up the menu from the coffee table in front of me.

"Oh my God, I'm so sorry! You asked what's good. But honestly, the chef will make whatever you want."

Huh, whatever I want? *Weird.* "So... if all I really wanted was some Vegemite toast, he'd be able to rustle that up for me?" I deadpan.

"Uh, um—sure, he'll do it. It might just take a little while. But if that's what you want, I'll pass it on to the chef." Shit, she looks nervous.

"I'm only joking. I don't want Vegemite toast. But it's interesting how far this place will go to serve the customer. Can I just have a ham and cheese toastie— oh, and the biggest chai latte you offer?'

"Ah, sure thing." I watch her write down my order, then she looks at me again. "So... a toastie is like... what, exactly?" Her eyebrows draw down in confusion.

"Oh, it's a toasted sandwich with ham and cheese on it. You know, I can just look at the menu and order something that's already on there."

"No, it's fine. That's what I thought it was—just wanted to make sure. Your order won't be long." Then, with a slight smile and a nod, she leaves me to my thoughts.

The tiny hairs on my neck prickle again. I feel as if

I'm being watched, but when I glance around, no one is paying me any mind. If anything, it looks like they're all desperately trying *not* to look my way.

My order comes out really quickly, especially considering how busy this place seems. Twenty minutes later, I'm ready to go back home, shower, make the bed, and sleep for another few hours.

"How was everything?" the same waitress asks when I approach the counter.

"That was probably the best toastie I've ever had." I smile. I'm telling her the truth. If toasties could have five stars, that would have been a five-star toastie.

"Oh, I'm glad. Here, before you go, this is for you too." She hands me a small white box.

"What is it?" I ask.

"Red velvet cake."

"Oh, I didn't order this." I try to hand it back to her, but she holds her palms up, refusing to accept it.

"I know you didn't. Someone else wanted you to have it. Thank you so much for dining with us. We hope to see you again soon."

"Uh, sure." I'm confused... Who would have ordered me cake? I don't know anyone here. I pull out my wallet, find a fifty, and hand it over to the waitress.

"I can't take that." She looks at my money like it has the ability to burn her.

"What do you mean? How much do I owe you? I don't think I have anything smaller." Surely fifty dollars is more than enough to cover my order.

"No, I meant you don't need to pay. Your meal was already covered." The waitress then turns around and walks out the back, leaving me more confused than ever.

I pull a pen and paper from my bag, and write down a little note. I don't know who thinks they can pay my tab, but I don't need anyone's money. I wrap the note around the fifty and leave it on the counter. Hopefully no one else takes it before the waitress returns.

The whole walk home I have that same prickly feeling, like someone is watching me. *Following me.* Yet, every time I turn around, no one is there. It freaks me out enough to quicken my strides. I make it back to my building in five minutes, locking the door and turning on every light in the empty apartment.

I spend the next few minutes pacing the small space, before deciding to shake the feeling off as simple paranoia. And the discomfort of being in a new city...

Chapter Three

"**Y**ou know I'm trying my fucking hardest to tune you the fuck out, right, Neo? And I can't do that when you're constantly yapping." I grunt at my cousin, who is also my second-in-command. Although, I may be on the hunt for his replacement in the very near future, if the son of a bitch didn't learn to shut the fuck up already.

As tempted as I am to pop a cap in his ass and

silence him for good, he's one of my best capos. That, and our *rules* say you can't shoot a made man just because you're sick of hearing his voice. Whoever the fuck thought that one up obviously hadn't met Neo.

There's also the fact that, despite his annoying-as-fuck personality, he's my best friend. The one person in this world I trust to have my back. *Always.* No matter how fucked up a situation gets, I know he'll be by my side, guns blazing. Fuck, the guy's so loyal he'd willingly follow me into the pits of hell and face off with the devil himself.

"Yeah, well, someone has to talk some fucking sense into that thick skull of yours. You're seriously going to tie yourself to her, to that family? For what? Because your papa says so? Fuck that. It ain't the fucking fifteenth century, man. Arranged marriages should not be a thing anymore," Neo yells, hitting the steering wheel with his open palm.

Why is he so fucking worked up over this? It's not like he's the one getting hitched to someone he's not even remotely attracted to. Don't get me wrong. Lana, my *fiancée*, is a knockout. Beautiful. *Model-worthy even.* The problem is... I've been friends with her since we were in diapers, and she's like my fucking sister.

As to why the fuck our fathers put this plan together, I have no idea. But my old man's the Don, and you don't say *no* to the fucking Don. It ain't a fucking option. So, like the dutiful son I am, the underboss, I set the example and follow my father's lead. *In everything*.

Besides, it could be worse. It could always be worse. At least that's what I tell myself... "My *papa* is the fucking Don. So, yeah, I'm gonna listen to him. Take the orders and follow through on this sham of a fucking marriage. Don't even try to tell me you'd do anything different."

"Of course I wouldn't. Believe it or not, I don't have a fucking death wish," he grumbles.

"Yeah, news flash, asshole. *Neither do I.* I just wish I knew what the fuck they're trying to achieve, by bringing the families together like this."

I don't understand why my father made this deal. Every time I've brought it up, he's blown me off with the usual nonsense of telling me it's time I settled down and started a family. That I need an heir. *Yeah, bullshit.* I'm fucking twenty-five years old. Why the fuck does he think I need an heir already? Maybe he's dying. If that's the case, I wish he'd do it before the nuptials. That way, I can kill the deal with Lana's family myself.

It's not that I don't love my father. *I do.* I even respect the hell out of him. He's always been someone I've looked up to, someone I've thrived to be like. My old man rules with an iron fist, a bloody one at that. But he's not just feared; he's respected among the men. I only hope I can be half the boss he is when it's my turn to lead the family.

Neo pulls up to the shopfront. "You ready to have

some fun?" he asks with a smile. The bastard is blood-thirsty. This is the part of the job I do because I have to. But Neo? He does it 'cause he fucking likes it. I think he gets off on the violence.

"As I'll ever be. Let's get this over with. I'm craving your sister's lasagna."

Neo laughs. "I should tell Aunt Gloria that you like Helena's lasagna better." He jumps out of the car, dodging the punch I was throwing his way.

"She would never believe you." I smirk. My mother thinks I'm a goddamn saint. I'm sure if you asked her, she'd even tell you the sun shone right out of my ass, and she'd believe it too. But she's Italian—most of our women are like that with their boys.

"I've got photo evidence of you eating at Helena's. A lot of it," he continues as we walk into the storefront. The little bell hanging above the door informs the occupants of our arrival.

It doesn't matter though. There's nowhere to run. *We'd find them.* If they're smart, they'll stay put and face us. If they're stupid, which they usually fucking are, they'll run and force me to chase them. And I don't fucking like playing cat and mouse—it never ends well for the rodent. Thankfully, these idiots seem to be the former. They stand there, their mouths gaping open like fucking fish out of water. If they don't pay up tonight, they might just be the fish *in* the water. With a brand-new pair of fucking cement shoes, courtesy of my father's men.

"Tsk, tsk, tsk. Neo, you know, I thought Luca and Paul here would have known better than to try to rip me off."

"Please, T, I didn't. I'll get you the money. We just need more time," Paul stutters out.

"You see, Paul, if I give you more time, then I gotta give Joe Blow down the street more time too. And then his cousin. And his fucking uncle. I'd never get paid. You can see how that'd be a problem for me, right?" I say as I fold up the sleeves of my white dress shirt.

"Please, we'll get you the money. I swear." Luca tries to plead their case this time.

"Mmm, I don't know, T. They seem genuine. Maybe we should give them a chance," Neo offers. He's a fucking psychopath, letting them think he's on their side right before he strikes. I see the flash of relief cross over their eyes. It doesn't last long. My cousin pulls his piece from his holster and shoots Paul's knee out. The fucker falls to the ground screaming. Meanwhile, Luca just stands there with his hands in the air. "*Or not.* We aren't known for being lenient, and I wouldn't want to wreck the Valentino name." Neo smiles.

"You're right. We're not, so why start now? We'll be back—same time tomorrow. Have my money, or it'll be more than just a knee. You got me?" I look to the trembling man.

"Y-yes, T. I'll have it." His whole body shakes from fear. At this point, I often wonder if I should feel empathy for these assholes. But then I remember that they borrowed money from the fucking mafia. If you don't want to end up in this situation, then go to a goddamn bank.

"See to it that you do. I don't like wasting my time." With that final message, I exit the shop, Neo following right behind me.

Thank God that's over. I'm fucking starving. "Let's go. I need to eat."

"Glad a bit of blood didn't make you lose your appetite."

"Shut up. It was one fucking time." I was also fucking fourteen. Any kid that age would throw up if they watched their father skin a man alive.

"One time too many, coz."

Stepping into Helena's café, I can tell something's off. I'm instantly put on high alert, and my pulse races. *What the fuck is going on?* Everyone knows this place is owned by Neo's sister. No one's stupid enough to mess with it.

I scan the interior. Everyone's quiet. As their eyes dart across the room, I recognize the fear, but they also look as though they're waiting for something. Like they're... curious. Then I spot the object of their curiosity.

A red-haired fucking angel. That's the only way I can describe the woman currently sitting in my fucking chair. The same chair that no one dares to occupy, because they know it's reserved for me. It's the best spot in the café. Right next to the fireplace with a view of the whole room.

My steps falter. I'm completely captivated by her. Then I remember everyone's still waiting on me, waiting to see what I'll do with the girl bold enough to sit herself in my chair. She's new. I've never seen her around here before. I'd remember if I had.

She's got her face buried in her phone, oblivious to the fact that all heads are currently turned in her direction. I can see that her lips are pursed, so maybe she's not that oblivious after all. But I can't see her eyes. I really want to see her fucking eyes.

"Torna a quello che stavi facendo. Chiunque tocchi quella ragazza mi risponderai." *Go back to what you were doing. Anyone who touches that girl will answer to me*, I tell them in my native Italian. Even if they don't understand me, everyone gets the message and the chatter resumes. "We'll eat in the office tonight. Make sure she gets whatever she wants, Helena." I don't wait for her reply. I know my cousin will do whatever I say. I walk through to the kitchen without a second glance towards the woman. As much as my whole body is aching to turn around, I don't.

Instead, I continue to the office, where I know I'll have a view of the whole café. Neo made sure there's a state-of-the-art CCTV system in place. I power on the wall of screens and sit on the lounge chair in front of the monitors.

I can't believe I'm about to say this. "Maybe you're right." I glance up at Neo, who hasn't said a word since we arrived.

"I usually am. But what, exactly, am I right about this time."

"I need to get out of this fucking marriage."

"And a certain cute little redhead you just left sitting in your spot—a spot you won't even let me sit in, *mind you*—has nothing to do with this change of heart, right?" he prompts.

"Or everything to do with it," I say absentmind-edly, as I watch her interact with Helena on the screen. The thing my cousin loves the most about the café business is interacting with the customers. She refuses to leave the floor, even though she makes more than enough to hire sufficient staff to wait the tables.

Half an hour later, I watch the red-haired vixen stand and head to the counter. I shoot to my feet, ready to follow her wherever she's going. I need to know where this woman lives. I need to know her name. *I need to know everything.*

I smile as I watch her leave a note by the register after Helena refused to take her cash. Pocketing the small piece of paper before walking out, I start making my way up the street. I keep to the shadows as I trail her steps.

She's smart though. She must sense she's being followed, because she picks up her pace. I stop across the street when she enters an apartment building. I wait. And then I see it. A light turns on, and she's looking out the window. It's like she's staring straight at me, but I know it's impossible. I'm too well hidden.

I pull the note from my pocket, finding a fifty-dollar bill wrapped around the paper. Is she nuts? She ate a grilled cheese, and she left fifty dollars?

I don't know how much I owe you, but hopefully this covers it.
Holly

Holly. I roll her name over my tongue. I like it. *I fucking love it.* I stand there and wait for her lights to turn off. Surely she'll be going to bed soon. Then images of her sprawled out over my sheets fill my fucking head. Fuck! I really need to find a way out of this engagement.

I watch for over an hour. Her lights never turn off, but she doesn't appear at the window again either.

Chapter Four

Holly

I wake to an insistent knocking. What the bloody hell is making all that noise? It takes a while but as I return to consciousness, I realize the pounding is coming from the front door. *Shit.* I get up, and as I head towards the sound, my feet freeze on the cold wooden floors beneath them. Why didn't I pack fluffy socks or something?

I'm praying it's not the creepy landlord. But no one

knows me here, so who else could it be? I peer through the peephole, and my breath catches. My heart races. Whoever is on the other side clearly has the wrong door.

The man—no, this guy is not just a man. He's more like a god. The phrase *Italian stallion* comes to mind as I stare at the creature just outside my apartment. He's wearing a dark-navy suit. Three pieces. With a vest and all. A very well-fitted suit, over a defined body. I'd like to see what that body looks like beneath the layers of clothing, because damn, does it look good in them. So, it can only look better out of them, right?

His mouth tips up at the corner. "Dolcezza, this is the part where you open the door," he says with a small laugh. That voice of his is lethal. Does he know what that tone does to a girl like me? I'm sure he does... How could he not? I'm surprised I'm still upright and not in a puddle on the floor.

Shit... He knows I've been standing here staring at him through the peephole. I can feel the heat rush up my neck to my face. I might as well get this mortification over with so I can climb back into bed.

I open the door and smile—a smile I don't quite feel. "Sorry, mate, you have the wrong apartment," I say, purposely inserting the Aussie slang. People here like Australians, at least that's what I've been told. Maybe he doesn't understand me? Is my accent that strong? Surely not.

Yet, the godlike creature stands there with a panty-melting smirk and a fire in his eyes I can't explain. But that gaze he's throwing my way as he looks me up and down is doing all kinds of things to my lady parts. Parts that have been lying dormant for a long, long time. Like I'd have to get out the cobweb duster to even find said parts at this point.

It hits me then—that I literally just got out of bed. I must look like a complete mess. I run my hands through my hair, trying my best to tame the long locks. I'm more self-conscious now than I've ever been in my whole life.

He tilts his head, stepping into the doorway but not crossing the threshold. I can't see past him into the hallway though; his body completely blocks me in. This is where I should feel fear. I should be shutting the door on this guy and locking it. However, I stand here, tilting my neck to look up at him like I'm lost in some sort of trance.

"You always answer your door dressed like that?" he asks.

"Huh?" *Yep, real intelligent answer, Holly.* What does he mean by *dressed like that*? My feet are bouncing a little as I try to ignore how cold my toes are. "Do you always knock on the wrong door?" I ask him in return, a little bit prouder of my response level this time.

"No, I've got the right one, dolcezza, but you should really put some more clothes on before you open your door to strangers. It's New York; there're a lot of weirdos around."

My insides heat up as he slowly drags his eyes down my body. *For a second time.* Holy shit, my legs involuntarily squeeze together. He notices. I can tell by the cocky-ass smirk he throws my way when his eyes finally meet mine again. This is where I wish I had just an ounce of Reilly's confidence. She'd be quicker with a comeback and put this guy in his place. Straightening my shoulders, while faking an arrogance that doesn't exist, I raise an eyebrow at him. "I can see that. Thanks for the warning." I shut the door on him, or at least I try to. He puts his foot forward to stop the impact.

And I have a moment of panic. This guy is huge. I wouldn't stand a chance against him if he tried anything. Shit, why the hell did I open the door? One night in New York, and I'm already going to end up on CNN or whatever news channel will report the horrific death of the idiot Aussie girl who opens her doors to strangers—he didn't even have to offer me candy or ask me to help him find his lost puppy.

"Fuck! Ah, here, this is for you. A little *welcome to New York* gesture." He lifts the offering towards my line of sight: a cardboard holder with a coffee cup, and a bag with the same logo on it as the café I stopped at last night.

How didn't I notice he was holding those? I might have been a little nicer just to get that black liquid gold from him. I take the proffered gifts. I'm so tempted to bring the cup to my lips—*tempted but not stupid.* Instead, I stare at the container, trying to figure out a way to tell if it's been drugged. For all I know, he could have roofied it or something.

Then one of his big hands reaches forward and plucks the coffee out of the tray. His mouth closes around the lid as he drinks. I now know it's possible to be jealous of a cup, because thoughts of those lips being wrapped around my nipples invade me.

"It's not tampered with, but you're smart for thinking twice about drinking it." His gravelly voice lulls me out of my own head. He returns the cup to the holder and takes a step back. "Lock the door behind me. Make sure you use the chain. I didn't hear you unlatch it."

I nod my head and shut the door; it's the only thing stopping me from utterly embarrassing us both by throwing myself at him. Leaning against the frame, I bring my hand to my chest. My heart is beating rapidly. What the hell was that? *Who* the hell was that? When he put his foot out barring me from slamming the door on him, I was scared. I could feel the panic attack coming on. Yet, at the same time, I was more turned on than I've ever been in my life.

"Holly, chain."

I let out a squeal. Shit, he's still there. My fingers stumble as they try to slide the chain into the latch. I finally get it on the third attempt. I look out through the peephole and watch his back as he slowly walks away.

Then I turn around and head towards the bedroom. It's not like I have any furniture to sit on in the living room anyway. Tucked back in the blankets, I reach into the coffee shop bag and pull out a chocolate chip muffin. A huge-ass muffin.

Whoever that man was, he can bring me coffee and muffins every morning. Raising the lid to my lips, I audibly sigh as the sweet caffeine hits my tongue, before balancing the cup between my legs. I reach back into the bag, looking for a napkin. I know I won't be able to bite into this muffin without dropping crumbs every-where. As I shake the napkins out, something drops onto my lap. Something I recognize. A fifty-dollar bill wrapped in a piece of paper. The same fifty-dollar bill I left on the counter at the café last night. But the note has someone else's handwriting on it now. Opening the folded square, I read the three simple lines:

Holly,
You left this behind.
Meet me for dinner. 7 p.m.

Yeah, that won't be happening. Did he follow me home? I turn the paper over, searching for a name.

There isn't one. As much as I want to insist I've managed to attract a psychopath on my very first night here, I can't seem to imagine him like that. I should be scared, but I remember how drawn I was to him.

His dark eyes looked downright dangerous, tormented even, and conflictingly comforting at the same time. I wanted to drown in them. Meet him for dinner? Where?

I laugh at myself for even considering *that* an option. There is no way I could do *that*. I couldn't even go out with a guy back home, not without dragging Reilly along with me under the guise of double dating. I'm not the daring sister. I'm the quiet one. The one who would rather be in bed and dream of being like my twin. I don't even have a friend here... someone I could force to come with me.

First dates and I don't do well together. But is that what the note is? A date invite? No, it can't be. Why would he want me to meet him for dinner? And where?

Nope, I can't do this. I crumple the note and throw it back into the paper bag. I am not letting myself get worked up over some guy, albeit some insanely hot guy, on my first day here. Nope, what I am going to do is get up, shower, and go furniture shopping.

The new Holly does not overthink things concerning the opposite sex. The new Holly will not obsess over whether I should or shouldn't meet Mr. Tall-Dark-And-Handsome for dinner. At seven o'clock tonight. God only knows where... I'm sure he means for me to meet him at the café; he obviously picked up the fifty-dollar note I left on the counter in order to return it.

Holy shit, he knew where I lived. It wasn't a random hot guy knocking on the wrong door. He came to see *me*—well, at least to deliver my money. Before I can even ask myself how the hell he knew where I lived, I know the answer. I knew I was being followed last night.

Those hairs on the back of my neck. The fuzzy sensation in the pit of my stomach. That same sensation I felt when the two men walked into the café last night. When *he* walked into the café last night... I'm blaming the lack of caffeine on the slowness of my brain, but it's finally catching up to speed. His voice, it's the same voice I heard speak Italian to everyone in the café.

Nope, I shake my head. I am not doing this. Shower and furniture shopping. *That's* what I'm doing today.

Chapter Five

The smile on my face feels somewhat foreign as I walk out of Holly's building. The strain in my pants? Not so much. But it's been a long time since I've gotten so fucking hard from just looking at a woman.

Holly's not like any of the women I've ever been with. She's different. Fucking beautiful, so damn beautiful it almost hurts to look at her. But there's something else about her too. I can't put my finger on it, but it's as if I'm pulled to her.

One word came to mind when she opened the door. *Mine.* That girl is mine. She doesn't know it yet; the world doesn't know it yet. But mark my words, heads will roll before I give her up.

"What the fuck is wrong with you?" Neo steps away from the blacked-out Escalade he was leaning against. I roll my eyes. Of course he's tracked me down. I swear the fucker's planted a GPS on me somewhere without my knowing. I've run a tracker-identifying device over every inch of my body and I've yet to find it. But he always manages to turn up wherever I am.

"What the hell do you want, Neo? It's eight in the morning. Shouldn't you be sleeping?"

"I would be, if my favorite cousin wasn't out doing God knows what. What exactly *are* you doing? Or should I say *who*? Because that weird-ass look you just had on your face is one I've never seen before, and I've seen all of your looks."

"Fuck off, Neo. I didn't have a look," I grunt.

"You had a look. Also, your papa has summoned us for an urgent meeting. Get in."

Neo jumps into the driver's side, and I head to the passenger's seat. "What does he want now?" I ask him. It's not unusual for my father to summon us for impromptu meetings; they just aren't ever at this hour of the morning. Honestly, I'd still be in bed if I didn't have a coffee to deliver and a hot-as-sin redhead to track down.

"No idea. Guess we'll find out soon." Neo shrugs and turns up the volume on the stereo, blasting some god-awful 90s rap song.

"Your taste in music is almost as bad as your taste in women," I grumble.

"Speaking of, how's the hottie from the café doin'?" The bastard laughs.

I briefly consider lying to him, telling him I have no idea who he's talking about, but there is no point. He knows me too well. "She's different," I answer, not really sure what else to say about her.

"*Different...* like you're about to start a fucking war just so you can have her? Or different like you're going to set her up in an apartment and visit her every other day?"

It's not unusual for the men in our family to have women on the side. But the thought of anyone treating Holly like *the other woman* has me seeing red. "I'll never have a side piece, Neo. You know this." My cousin knows where I stand on infidelity. It's not an option for me. I've watched my mother's heart break over and over again every time my father didn't return home for days at a time. I'll never do that to my own wife.

"So, it's going to be the war option. Good... things have been getting a bit boring around here lately." Neo grins like the psychopath he is.

"There's not going to be a fucking war. I'll figure a way out of this marriage with Lana. *Without inciting bloodshed.* I just have to determine what my father is getting out of the exchange and provide a better offer."

"Uh-huh, sure. Just so you know, if you can't do it peacefully, I'm all for a blood bath and taking over the world. All that shit. My loyalties lie with you, T. No one else."

"I know. And I appreciate it, but don't let the current Don hear you say that."

Fifteen minutes later, we pull into my family's estate. *Here goes nothing.* Visiting your parents should not induce anxiety; I'm pretty sure it's meant to be a pleasant, warm feeling. But ever since my father dropped that whole arranged marriage crap on me, I haven't wanted to come here. All I can think is: *what the fuck does he want from me now?*

I grew up idolizing the man. Aside from how he stepped out on my mom, he was a good father. He showed me the ways of the family, taught me everything I know about being a leader, being a boss. I just didn't realize how much of my life he had planned out for me from the moment I entered this world. I was born to be his heir, to fill a role. And fill it I did. Exceedingly well. I was the youngest made man in the family. Conducted my first kill when I was only twelve.

But the old man's crazy if he thinks I'll silently sit by and go along with this wedding shit now. Before

Holly appeared, I was prepared to do what I had to—*if* it meant doing what was best for the family—even if I wasn't happy about going in blind. That being said, I should really question my own sanity... I'm ready to spill blood in order to have a woman I know absolutely nothing about. No, in order to have a *chance* with her.

I need to rectify that problem. Before I walk into my parents' home, I send off a quick text to my investigator. This guy will get me everything I need to know about my mystery girl. All I have to do is give him her first name and address with the instruction of leaving no stone unturned.

Putting my phone back into my pocket, I inhale deeply before straightening out my jacket and walking into the place like I own it—which I guess, in a way, I do. All of this will be mine when I take over my father's role.

"Good morning, Mr. Valentino. Your father is in his office. He's expecting you." Teresa, the family's housekeeper, greets me in the foyer.

"Thank you, Teresa." I nod my head and make my way to the office with Neo right behind me.

Knocking once, I wait until I hear the command. "Enter." I roll my eyes before turning the handle. My father, a man of few words.

I school my features as I walk in, refusing to display an ounce of my internal shock (or stress) over seeing who else is in the room.

"Good morning." I greet everyone as I take in my

surroundings; it's a necessary evil. You can never be too careful when it comes to an ambush. I've collected my fair share of enemies over the years—those who would love nothing more than to take me out—and I refuse to make that task easy for the fuckers.

I don't sit. Instead, I walk over and stand next to where my father is positioned behind his obnoxiously large mahogany desk. I make eye contact with Lana, hoping to gauge the situation from her. There's a slim chance she already knows what this meeting's about, although the stress in her eyes tells me she's just as clued in as I am.

"Right, now that we're all here, we can get down to business," my father says, while giving me a side-eye that orders me to keep my mouth shut.

Unfortunately for Neo, he's not as equipped at reading the room, or at the very least, he chooses not to be. "And what business would that be, boss?" he asks. My father doesn't answer him. He does however send daggers his way, which Neo shrugs off.

"We are here to set a date. This engagement has gone on long enough. We thought we were doing right by allowing things to progress naturally between the two of you and letting you handle the arrangements. But it's come to our attention that you're both dragging your heels for reasons we will not discuss today. We will, however, set the date. That's the very least we have to give to the planner." My father leans back in his chair.

Fuck! Shit! No fucking way. Set a date? I look to Lana, and she appears as though she's going to be sick. Her skin pales. I can see her heart race, and her breathing picks up. I know Lana better than she knows herself, and right now, she's either about to run to the bathroom in tears or go batshit crazy and start cussing out two of the five bosses of New York.

Neither are a permissible option at the moment. I need time. If I'm going to get the both of us out of this, I need more time. But if Lana says anything now, they'll know we don't want to go through with this shit. I need everyone to think we are all in.

"Lana and I already set a date. We were going to invite the families to dinner next week to discuss it," I declare, making my way around the desk to my would-be bride before picking her up and embracing her. Leaning down, I kiss her cheek and whisper, "Get it together, L. Do not say a thing. Just nod your head and go along with it."

Her eyes meet mine, and she gives the subtlest nod, letting me know she'll follow my lead.

"You set a date? For when?" This comes from John, Lana's father. He's a bastard and probably the least respected boss out of the crowd. However, he is still a boss. And, for right now at least, he's also my future father-in-law.

So, instead of telling the son of a bitch to fuck off and get the fuck out of my family's house, I play nice. "Five months' time. We thought February 14th would

46

be fitting." Fuck knows where I pulled that date from, but everyone seems pleased with my choice.

"Great, I'll let the wedding planner know. Now, if that's settled, I have more pressing things to do. Dinner next week at your place, T, sounds like a great way to make the date announcements to the rest of the family." My father stands, signaling the end of the meeting.

"Actually, Theo, I wanted to have dinner at my place. It'll be one of the last chances I'll have to host, you know, before I move in." Lana catches me by surprise. She's never willingly spoken out at any of these fucked-up meetings—and there has been more than a few of them.

"Ah, yeah, Pops, L has it all planned already. Let's meet at her place on Wednesday." I wait for my father's response. As much as I'd love to just take Lana and walk the fuck out of this office, I can't turn my back on him until he responds. It would be disrespectful to do anything else. Thankfully, he doesn't make me wait too long before I can make my hasty exit.

"Sure, why not? See you then."

I nod. Placing my hand on Lana's lower back, I lead her out of the room. Once the door is shut, I raise my finger to my lips telling her to keep quiet. Neo is right behind us as he exhales as loudly as he possibly can. "Well, looks like I need to get my tux dry cleaned, huh?"

"Shut it, asshole," I grit out as I lead Lana to the car. I close her in the back before jumping into the passenger's seat. I don't say a word until Neo has pulled out of the gates. "What the fuck was that? Did you know that was happening?" I turn my glare on Lana. I know she doesn't deserve to bear the weight of my wrath right now. But, fuck, I'm beyond pissed.

"First off, you can take that glare somewhere else; it doesn't work on me. Second, if I knew they were planning that ambush, I would have warned you," she seethes, before slumping back in the seat.

"We're not getting married, L," I say out loud for the first time.

"No shit, we're not. I'd rather welcome an untimely death than be sentenced to a life as your wife." She physically shakes, like the thought of being with me is unimaginable, then adds, "No offense."

"Yeah, none taken. I need you to not do anything rash. *Or stupid.* I'll figure a way out of this mess, without anyone dying in the process. Any idea what your father's getting out of it?"

"Not a damn clue. I've searched every scrap of paper in his office, his safe. Nothing. I'm coming up empty."

"There has to be something. We just need to find out what. Someone has to know."

"Have you—oh, I don't know—tried asking your father?" Lana retorts. I don't bother answering her. Instead, I tell Neo to drop her off at her apartment. "T, not that I'm complaining, but why the sudden change of heart? I mean, up until today, you've been willing to go along with this bullshit idea?"

"No reason in particular. I just don't want to spend the rest of my life eating your food, L." I smirk and dodge the tiny fist swinging towards my head.

"Well, prepare yourself, because next week's dinner will be to die for." Lana smiles and opens the door, right as the car comes to a stop outside her apartment building.

Chapter Six

Holly

"Shit!" The two bags in my right hand drop to the floor as I attempt to get the key in the door. *Live in an apartment*, they said. *It's the New York way of life*, they said. Well, whoever *they* are, they're bloody idiots. I've been back to my new apartment three times today, each trip with arms full of shopping bags.

Starting from scratch is a lot more work than I

anticipated. But day one: I've managed to fully stock the kitchen. I'm sure once I start unpacking the bags I'm going to feel much better about this whole *starting fresh* thing.

But first, I need a shower. I need to get into some comfy pjs and the new pair of pink fluffy socks I snagged today. Before I head to the bathroom, I put the bottle of white wine—the one I just couldn't walk past —in the freezer to chill. I'm hoping by the time I'm done in the shower I can order some food, drink wine, and unpack my kitchen appliances and utensils.

The hot water running over my back is exactly what I needed. As I lather the coconut-scented suds over my body, my mind drifts to the person I've tried my darndest not to think about today. I haven't allowed myself to remember how his broad shoulders filled out his jacket. The way his eyes lit a trail of butterflies and tingles all over my skin when they roamed up and down my body.

My fingertips trace along my neck, then to the middle of my chest before continuing towards my belly button. Nope, I did not think of the cocky smirk he formed as one corner of his mouth tipped up, almost like he was fighting a smile. Or his voice, that gravelly deep tone that went straight through me. No, I didn't think about how my vagina begged to be touched when he said my name through the closed door. My hand travels lower to the lips of my core. Spreading them apart, my fingers slowly circle my clit.

"Mmm." My head falls back, hitting the tiled wall. It's as if my insides have been strained all day, waiting for a release. Inserting two fingers, I slowly pump them in and out while I press my palm against my clit. "Oh fuck." I wish this was *his* hand. I wish his mouth was traveling over every inch of my body.

My other hand cups my left breast, pinching the nipple as I imagine what it would be like to have his mouth latched on to it. My fingers pick up their speed. I'm chasing that high, and it's so close. Shutting my eyes, I conjure up his image in my mind: tall, broad, tanned. *Smoking fucking hot is what he is.*

Staring right into his dark eyes—or at least how I envision them—I reach my peak. My thighs clamp together. And I come. Falling to the floor, I realize there is no way I can see this man again. I just got myself off to the memory of him. How can I possibly face him now? It's a good thing I never intended to accept that dinner invite.

Two glasses of wine later, I've ordered in a heap of Chinese food and my kitchen is—well, frankly, it's a mess. But it's getting there. Oh, and bonus: I've hardly thought about a certain tall-dark-and-handsome stranger. I'm sure by now he's gotten the point that I won't be showing up for his dinner invite, not that he left an actual meeting place on his note.

I dial Reilly—if anyone can take my mind off things, it's my sister. Sitting the phone on a box on the bench, I wait for the video call to connect.

"Holly, thank God you're alive and haven't been— oh, I don't know—stabbed, mugged, or worse, since you're now living in the most dangerous city in the world." Reilly worries too much. Is this how every call is going to go from now on? My twin, needing proof of life?

"That's a little dramatic, even for you. Where's Bray? Someone needs to rein you in."

"I'm here, and you and I both know there is no *reining in* your sister." Bray's face fills the screen before Reilly moves the phone back to hers.

"He's just leaving for the gym." I watch as Bray takes hold of her jaw and kisses her like it's the last time. My heart aches. I'm not jealous of my sister. *I'm envious of what she has.*

I want a love so deep that I feel it in every tiny cell in my body. I want a love that conquers all. A love that withstands the test of time. I want what *they* have. I wonder if I'm destined to be the spinster sister.

"Chat later, twin two. Things to do; people to see. Be safe." Bray waves as he heads out the door.

"I do love to watch that man walk away." Reilly sighs.

"Eww, no, Rye. Just no."

"Okay, enough about my hunky hubby. Let's talk about you. How has the first day or so been?"

"Uh, eventful," I say as my mind drifts where it shouldn't.

"Shut the front door! Holly Reynolds, who is he, and how is it that you've met someone already?"

"Don't be stupid. I haven't met anyone, Rye. I'm just tired. As you can see, I've spent the whole day shopping and the night unpacking, trying to jam as much as I possibly can into this pathetically small excuse for a kitchen." I wave the phone around to show her the progress—or should I say *the mess*.

"Jeez, Hol, did you buy out the whole of Walmart?"

"Well, considering I didn't even have so much as a teaspoon here, yeah, I probably did buy out the whole of Walmart." The sound of someone banging on the door interrupts whatever smartass response Reilly was going to say. "Hold that thought—that's my dinner and I'm starving," I yell a little too excitedly. I place the phone back down on the counter.

"Wait, position the screen so I can see the door... you know, just in case the delivery driver is a crazy axe murderer."

"You're literally on the other side of the world. What could you even do?"

"Call 9-1-1?" she questions.

I consider this, deciding that having someone to call the cops (on the off chance I'm about to get murdered) is better than nothing. I turn the phone around so Reilly has a good view of the doorway. "Okay, but if I die, I want my ashes scattered over the library from *Beauty and the Beast*." I laugh.

"That doesn't actually exist, Hol. Just answer the door, so we can get back to talking about your hopeless homemaking skills."

"Fine, but my homemaking skills aren't hopeless," I say, as I swing the door open just as another loud knock sounds out through the room. "H..." My mouth loses the ability to speak the rest of my greeting. I'm standing in my doorway—in my pjs and pink fluffy socks—staring at the one person I've been doing my best to avoid. *To not even think about.* What is *he* doing here?

"Are you okay, sweetheart?" His hand comes up and rests on my forehead. He's touching me... Why is he touching me?

"Ah, Hol, WTF. Why the bloody hell don't our Uber Eats drivers look like *that*? Is it an American thing?" Reilly's voice breaks me out of my stupor.

"Um, what are you doing here?"

"You didn't show up to dinner." I wait for him to explain further. He doesn't.

"So, you what? Thought you'd come knock on my door for...?"

"First, to make sure you were okay. Second, to have dinner with you, of course." He holds up bags of takeout.

"Right. Sorry, I've already eaten," I lie. I cannot be alone with this man.

"You'll have to try harder than that, dolcezza. I got here just as your delivery driver pulled up. *This* is the food *you* ordered."

"What happened to the driver? I haven't paid for that yet. Hold on, let me get my purse." Without thinking, I walk back to the kitchen and rummage through the mess on the bench. I turn with a start when I hear the door close behind me. *Shit.* Instinctively, I back up, my heart racing as my panic increases. He's in my apartment. In my apartment, where the only exit's blocked... by him.

How the hell did I get myself into this situation? I look around. Maybe there's a window I can climb through. A fire escape?

"Cazzo, dolcezza, you're okay. I'm not going to hurt you. It's just dinner." The guy walks towards me, placing the bags on the counter.

"Ah, Holly, I have 9-1-1 already dialed. Need me to connect the call?" Reilly prompts.

Shit, I forgot she was still on video chat. "No, I'm okay." I walk around the counter and pick up the phone. "Rye, I'm going to call you back later."

"No, you don't. Who the hell is the hottie in the suit wanting to have dinner with you? Hol, you've been in New York for what? A day? And you've got a man *like that* already lining up for you?"

"Don't be ridiculous. I don't have any men lining

up for me, idiot. Bye, love you. Chat later." I hang up the call before she can respond. I've already embarrassed myself enough in front of *the hottie in a suit*.

And I'm still not sure if I should be looking for a quick escape. Or maybe a weapon...

Chapter Seven

Hearing Holly say she doesn't have men lining up for her is music to my ears. But the fact that she's currently looking for an escape route (or perhaps a method of bludgeoning me) is disconcerting, to say the least.

This woman is one of the few people I don't want to fear me. "You don't need to be afraid. I'll never hurt you, Holly."

She stares at me blankly for a while. I watch as she picks up a glass of wine from the bench, swallowing half the contents in one go. "I'm sure that's what all the crazy axe murderers say right before they kill their prey."

"I can assure you: I am no crazy axe murderer. Though you may, in fact, be my prey of a different kind."

"What kind of prey?" she prompts.

"The kind I want to keep and make mine." Holly's eyes widen in shock, her mouth gapes, and all I can think of is sliding my cock between those plump lips of hers. The last thing I need is a fucking hard-on while I'm trying to convince her I'm not some kind of weirdo. "So, ah, do you have plates, or do you just wanna eat from the cartons?" I ask as I pull the food from the bag. It looks like she's ordered enough to feed the entire complex.

"Um, I have plates, but I was planning on eating straight from the cartons, so I didn't have to wash dishes. Not sure if you noticed, but the kitchen is in shambles at the moment." She starts picking up empty boxes and stacking them in neater piles on the opposite side of the bench.

"I didn't notice. Okay, let's go sit and eat." I take all five cartons, the chopsticks, and a handful of napkins over to the empty living room and sit down cross-legged on the floor. Holly watches me from the kitchen making no move to come join my makeshift picnic. "Come and sit. You must be starving."

"What makes you think I'm starving?" she asks as she lowers herself down in front of me.

"The fact that you ordered enough food to feed a small country?" I shrug.

"I just couldn't make up my mind." She peeks into the open containers and picks up a box of honey chicken and rice. "You know, it's bloody rude to invite yourself over for dinner and eat my food."

"I invited *you* to dinner, and *you* stood me up."

"That doesn't mean you can invite yourself here. Usually, when a girl doesn't show up, it's because she probably doesn't want to have dinner with you."

"Huh, is that what it means? It's never happened before so I wasn't sure. Thanks for clearing that up for me." I grab a box of some kind of beef stir-fry and take a bite. "So, why is it exactly that you didn't want to have dinner with me?"

Holly coughs on the food she was chewing. "I... um... I don't do very well on first dates. Not that I thought your invite was a date or anything. I just... I don't do dinner, well, with men."

"It's a date, Holly. And it seems to me like you're doing dinner with a man right now."

"This is not a date; this is you barging your way into my home and eating my food." She smiles.

"All right, let me take you on a real date then —tomorrow."

"Mmm, I'll think about it."

"Okay. So, how do you like New York so far?" I ask her.

"How do you know I'm new to New York?"

Shit, I can't tell her that I had her investigated. "Lucky guess. You have no furniture in your apartment and you're unpacking what looks like every kitchen utensil known to mankind."

"Well, tomorrow is furniture shopping day. Today was kitchen day. I can live without a couch, but I cannot live without a stocked kitchen."

"Where did you move from?"

"Sydney," she says, though I already know the answer.

"Why New York?"

"Ah, no. It's my turn. I don't even know your name? Who are you and what do you do?"

"I'm Theo Valentino. I'm an entrepreneur." I hold my hand out to shake hers. It was a mistake, because the moment her soft hand clasps mine, little shocks run up my arm. I wrap my palm around hers and bring it to my mouth, placing a light kiss on her wrist before letting her go. I want to kiss every creamy inch of her skin. I want to lick and bite and mark her as mine.

"I'm Holly, but you already know that."

"Well, Holly, it's nice to meet you. So, what brings you to New York?" I ask again.

"I just wanted a fresh start, something different.

Have you ever felt like you were hidden in the shadows, and you just couldn't find your way out?"

"More than you could possibly know."

"Well, that was my life in Sydney. Don't get me wrong, it wasn't horrible, just... boring. Predictable. Plus, my sister got married and is starting her new life with her husband. I didn't want to be the third wheel anymore."

"Are you close with your sister?"

"Very—we're twins. Probably couldn't get much closer. That was her. Before. On the phone."

"That would explain why she looked so much like you. Any other siblings?" I ask, already knowing the answer, but it seems like the next natural question. Besides, hearing about her life *from her* is far more informative than reading about it in a report. How much will she tell me? What parts will she hold back? Does her past still inflict pain? Why is she really here? None of that can be conveyed by a piece of paper.

"A brother, Dylan. He passed away a few years ago." Her eyes glass over with a sudden sadness.

"I'm sorry." I've been around death for as long as I can remember, yet I can't for the life of me figure out the right words to comfort Holly. I know from the report I received earlier that her brother died in a car accident at the fault of a drunk driver. I also know that her father is currently incarcerated for killing the fucker behind the wheel. I need to figure out who we have in Sydney to get her father out. No man should be in jail for defending his own.

"It's not your fault. It's okay. Anyway, it's been just Reilly, me, and Mum for a while now... so to be here alone is a little overwhelming. But I'm standing by my choice."

"What about your dad? Where is he?" I ask, wondering if she'll make something up or not.

"He's... um... He's in jail. Back home. What about you, any siblings?"

I love that she was honest. I can tell it's not an easy topic for her, so I'll let her change it. "No siblings. Guess my folks got it right the first time and didn't see a need to go back for more." I laugh.

"Right. I'm sure that's why you're an only child."

"So, what do you plan to do in New York?"

"I start my new job in a couple of weeks. Until then, I plan to furnish this place and turn it into a home."

"You slept here last night with no furniture?" I ask.

"I have a bedroom set. The landlord let me have it delivered ahead of time."

"That's good."

Holly and I spent over an hour eating and talking. Asking questions back and forth. I don't think I've ever talked to a woman like this. It's nice, but it's getting late and I can see she's tired. "Here, let me pack this away and I'll get out of your hair." I stand and hold my hand out for her to take. She hesitates slightly before placing a palm in mine and letting me pull her up.

"This is by far the best first non-date I've ever had," I tell her honestly.

"This wasn't a date. If it were, I'm sure you would have found a reason to leave a long time ago. I don't date well, remember?"

"Maybe you just weren't going on dates with the right person. There is nothing about you that's making me run for the door. Believe me, Holly, I wouldn't bother looking for a reason to leave. If I didn't want to be here, I'd simply walk out."

"That's oddly sweet, considering how dickish that made you sound." Holly laughs, and it's fucking melodic. What the fuck is wrong with me...? To have me thinking her laugh sounds like a symphony?

I finish loading the leftover food containers into her fridge. Turning back around, I see that Holly is holding her phone while tapping away at the keys. Without looking up, she apologizes. "Sorry, it's Reilly. If I don't answer her, she'll have the swat team or something breaking the door down."

"It's okay. You can call your sister back. Tell her all

about the charming date you just had. I gotta head out anyway. I'll see you tomorrow."

"This wasn't a date, and I haven't agreed to go on a date with you tomorrow either."

I choose to ignore her noncompliance. It doesn't matter to me, seeing as one way or another, we will be having dinner together tomorrow night. So, instead of correcting her, I lean in and kiss her forehead.

"See you tomorrow, dolcezza. Lock the door after me, and use the chain," I instruct, before walking over to the door and opening it. I look back to see Holly positioned exactly how I left her. "Holly, lock the door. Please." I add the *please* at the end to try to soften the abrasive tone.

"Ah, sure. Thank you for the non-date."

"You're late," Neo states the obvious from the sidewalk.

"Had shit to do." I'm not about to tell him I was late because, frankly, I'd rather be holed up in Holly's empty apartment right now than doing my father's dirty work.

"Does that *shit* have anything to do with a certain red-headed beauty?" He stomps out his cigarette butt with his boot.

"You know, that shit's going to catch up and kill you one day." I nod towards the ground.

"Yeah, somehow I think my job will get me way before any cancer stick." He shrugs.

"Try to avoid that for as long as possible. I don't want to have to recruit a new underboss when I take over the family."

"Don't worry, T, I'm indestructible. Now, let's go do some damage, because there is no way these fuckers have our fucking money."

"Let's get this shit over with."

We walk into the shop where both brothers are standing behind the counter. I can't see their hands. I don't fucking like the idea of having a gun pulled out on me tonight, so I'm quick to draw my own. Then, without a second thought, I put a hole right through the head of the older brother, Luca. Paul's screams fill the room, and I see the glint of metal in his hand. If this fucker thinks he's going to get the best of me, he can fuck right off with that.

My gun fires and he slumps over in shock, the bullet hitting his shoulder and sending his weapon to the floor. "Fuck you, Valentino. I'm going to fucking kill you, you son of a bitch," Paul yells his empty threats.

"And here I was, considering letting you live... then you had to go and call my mother a bitch."

"He could have been calling your father a bitch too?" Neo adds.

"You're right." I cross my arms as if deliberating.

"Should we dial the boss and let him know what Paul here thinks of him?"

"I don't know, Neo... Pops hates being interrupted when he's busy."

"Yeah, we probably shouldn't bother him with this, not when we can deal with it ourselves." Neo smirks at me before turning to face Paul. "So, I'm going out on a limb here... but I'm guessing you don't have our money."

"I've got it—well, I'll have it. I-I swear I'll get it. I just need more time."

"That, my friend, is a luxury we just don't have." I'm not wasting my breath on this idiot anymore. I point my gun at his head and pull the trigger. "Get a clean-up crew here. I've got shit to do."

"No problem. You headed to Helena's for dinner?"

"Nah, I've already eaten." I'm not hanging around and giving Neo the chance to ask me the fifty thousand questions he has swirling around in that brain of his. I exit the building and make my way down the street.

As I stroll along the darkened sidewalk, avoiding the glow of the streetlights, Holly's words from earlier seep into my thoughts: *Have you ever felt like you were hidden in the shadows, and you just couldn't find your way out?*

Chapter Eight

Holly

After a grueling sixty-minute phone call to Reilly, I was left tossing and turning all night. Going over everything that was said in the conversation I had with him. I've never met a man I could talk to so easily, so openly. Like I'd known him for years, not mere hours.

Theo had this way of making me feel calm—safe even—which is something I'm not overly accustomed to lately. That was part of the reason for my move here: everywhere I went in Sydney I was looking over my shoulder, waiting for that crazed madman to make another entrance. It's an irrational fear. I know the guy who shot Bray is no longer able to hurt anyone. But the fear is there nonetheless.

Last night, the initial shock of Theo inviting himself in and closing the door drew that same fear to the surface, to the point that I was considering making a run for the window. Once Theo spoke though, his body language and actions reassured me that I was safe with him.

I could very well be delusional, led into a false sense of security before he shows his true colors. Perhaps that's still to come. But if I were to judge Theo solely on how he was last night, I would say he's the perfect gentleman, albeit a little forward.

Okay, a lot forward. I recall him telling me I was his prey and that he intended on making me his. I wonder what that entails exactly, and if being *his* is something I should be wanting at all.

Although I felt safe with him, there was a darkness in his eyes that I couldn't quite put my finger on. I was drawn to it, drawn to him, but that's ridiculous. I must still be suffering from jet lag or something, because I've never in my life felt a connection like I had with Theo. It's different from what Reilly and I share, of course.

The kind of connection I felt with Theo last night is the one I've been searching for my whole adult life, yet the exact one I'm terrified of acknowledging. I wonder if this is how Reilly felt when she first met Bray. She did not give into her feelings for him easily. I knew she was fighting it, but in the end, they both got their happily ever after.

Is Theo mine? My forever?

Probably not, but that doesn't mean he can't be my happily right now. As it stands, I know absolutely no one in New York, so to think at the very least I've made one friend is comforting. Maybe this really will be a great year. Maybe I can find the new me here. It may not be with Theo, but damn, I could imagine finding out a lot of new things about myself with that man.

Flipping the blankets off, I decide to jump straight in the shower and make an early start on the furniture shopping adventures ahead of me. I'd love to be able to come home to a couch—a dining table to eat at wouldn't go astray either.

By the time I get to the sidewalk, the sun is up and people are out on the street mingling around and going about their day. I breathe in the cool air and tighten my jacket around my body. As I walk down the street, I tell myself that I'm going to Helena's for the amazing coffee I'm in desperate need of. I'm most certainly not going there on the off chance I'll run into anyone in particular. It occurred to me at some point between showering and getting dressed that I have no way to contact him. Even if I wanted to see him again, I wouldn't be able to make those plans.

I guess the ball's in his court; he was insistent that we'd be having dinner again tonight. I'm not opposed to the idea, but I'm also trying to be a realist. I don't want to get all caught up on this guy, only to have him not show.

Like I did to him last night... Shit, now I feel guilty.

I push through the doors of the café and look around. The place is mostly empty, compared to how filled it was during my first visit.

"Holly, good morning. What can I get for you?" The same lady who was working two nights ago greets me.

"You must be good with names, to remember mine. I'm sorry I didn't catch yours?"

"I'm Helena." I'm about to hold my hand out to shake hers when her arms wrap around me in a tight hug. Okay, I guess we're hugging... I return her embrace, though awkwardly. "I'm so excited. I'm glad you came back. Here, come sit. What can I get you?" She ushers me over to the counter before gesturing to a booth.

"Um, can I just get the largest cup of chai latte you can manage, please?" I ask.

"Sure, won't be long."

"Ah, Helena, mind if I go sit on the couches by the fire?"

The look she gives me tells me she wants to say no. But then she smiles and nods her head. "Sure, I'll bring your coffee over to you, hun."

"Thanks." I make myself comfortable in the same single wingback chair, which had offered me reprieve on that first night. I slip my shoes off and tuck my feet under my legs.

I'm deep in my list of items I want to purchase today and googling different furniture shops in the neighborhood, by the time Helena comes out with my coffee. She deposits the steaming mug on the table in front of me. "Here you go."

"Thank you." I place the notepad and pen down and pick up the cup. "Mmm, this is bloody good. I needed this."

"I'm glad you like it. Let me know if there's anything else I can get you."

After a few sips of the liquid gold, I dive back into my list. The more I think about what I need, the longer the list gets. It's all becoming a little overwhelming. I'm not even sure where to start.

I check the time on my phone. Maybe I should call Reilly or my mum, and get some advice? I know... I'm the twenty-something-year-old who chose to stay at home, instead of moving out.

And, of course, I had to choose a foreign country as my first excursion, with no friends or family support. What the hell was I thinking? I can't do this. Why did I think I could do this by myself?

I feel my eyes forming the tears. But I force them to remain at bay. *I will not cry. I will not lose my shit in public*—it's become a new mantra or so it seems. I take in a calming breath, and that's when I feel it.

That's when I feel *him*. He's here. I don't even have to look up to know he's here. It would be super weird of me to just throw my arms around him and make him hug me right now. But that's exactly what I want to do.

I want the feeling of his arms around me. Yet, I don't turn around. I don't run and jump him like the weirdo that I am. No, I just sit here, trying hard not to let the tears fall. I stare at my phone, willing it to ring. Have a message pop up. Anything to distract me from my own mind would be good.

I see his shiny black shoes stop in front of me. I don't lift my head. Shit, why didn't I just hightail it out of here when I felt his presence? One look at my watery eyes, and he's going to know I'm weak. He will know I'm not who he thought I was. I'm not some strong, independent woman who can leave her whole life behind to start a new one in a city nothing like her own.

Theo sits down on the coffee table right in front of me. I want to look up, to acknowledge that he's there, but I just need another minute to make sure I can plaster on the happy face he deserves to see. He doesn't wait for me. He places his fingers under my chin, raising my eyes. I feel his lips touch my forehead, and I melt into him. How can a single touch make me feel like this? Warm and comforted. No words needed. Just a single touch, and it's as if everything is going to be okay.

"Good morning, dolcezza." His eyes travel along my face before they harden. "What's wrong? Who the fuck made you cry?" The harsh tone jolts me back. I was expecting him to be confused, or to find an excuse to make a hasty escape. But not the anger...

"Um, nothing. I'm just tired—that's all. You know, this whole jet lag thing is a bitch." I try to shrug it off.

"Holly, you're a shitty liar, but we'll work on that. Right now, I want you to tell me what's actually wrong?"

"I'm not a shitty liar. And I'm fine. A little over-whelmed, maybe. I don't know... It's just hit me that I've moved across the bloody world with no family. No friends. I'm suddenly alone for the first time in my whole life. I guess it's just more than I expected. I was making a list of all the things I need to go and get today and... I don't know... It's just... *a lot.*" *Way to act cool, Holly.* I don't know how he does it, but he makes me spill everything I'm holding inside, and I actually feel a little better now that I got it out to someone.

"Okay." He takes both of my hands in his. "First, you're not alone. You have me. Second, where's your list? How about we tackle it together?"

"Oh, no, you don't have to waste your time shop-ping with me. I'll be fine, really. I'm sorry to put all of that on you. I was just having a moment. But I'll be fine. It's just furniture shopping. It's not like it's hard.

You just go about whatever it is you do. And I'm going to finish my coffee, order another one to go, and get stuck into a day of shopping." Theo picks up my notebook and takes a picture of the list of shops I jotted down. "What are you doing?" I ask, confused.

"Sending my driver our intended stops for today. You finish your coffee. And I'll ask Helena to make you another one to go." He's up and walking over to the counter before I can think of a response. He's not seriously going to spend the day furniture shopping with me, is he? Why would he do that?

Chapter Nine

When I saw the tears forming in Holly's eyes, I wanted blood. I've never felt a rage so fierce; the thought that someone had upset her pissed me the fuck off. I wanted to be her dark knight, avenging her honor.

Then, when I discovered she was just overwhelmed with everything, I wanted to be her white knight, solving all of her problems and taking the burden from her shoulders.

I had a list of jobs to do today, which I'm now passing off to Neo, all because I can't seem to leave Holly when I know she's struggling. If I don't fix this for her, she could very well jump on a plane home.

At this point, I'd follow her, just to bring her back here anyway. I haven't felt this possessive—this protective—over anyone before. And it's fucking unsettling. I'm not about to ignore it though; something tells me it's a once in a lifetime sort of thing.

"Helena, can you make Holly a coffee to go?" I ask distractedly as I text Neo.

"Sure, but don't think you're getting away with this that easily, T. What's going on with you two?" Helena is the family gossip—and by now, I'm sure all the cousins and aunts know that Holly exists.

"You have to keep your lips sealed about this one, Helena," I warn her. The last thing I want is word getting back to my fucking father. "I mean it. She's important, and I just need time to sort shit out before I bring her into the family."

Helena's eyes widen at my words. "What about Lana?"

"What about her? You know, as well as I do, that L and I will only end up killing each other if we have to go through with this shit."

"Okay, I won't say anything. But not for you. I

happen to like Holly. She's a breath of fresh air."
Helena walks away.

My phone goes off with messages from Neo asking, in his words exactly: *what I'm doing that's so important I need him to cover for my sorry ass.* But I choose to ignore him.

I approach Holly as she's packing her notebook and pen into her bag. She stands and turns right into me, stumbling back a step. I reach out a hand to steady her. "I knew I'd get you to fall for me eventually." I laugh.

"Like you'd even have to try." Holly inches away, effectively untangling herself from my hold. "I'm just going to go and pay for my coffee. You really don't need to waste your day shopping with me, you know."

"Trust me, dolcezza, I have purely selfish reasons for wanting to spend the day with you. Are you ready to get out of here?" I ask, taking hold of her palm.

Holly looks down at our now conjoined hands and then back up at me. "Ah, yeah, let me just stop at the counter first."

"There's no need. It's been taken care of." In the past, most girls loved it when I paid for their shit for them. Holly is not like most girls...

Nope, she doesn't look the least bit impressed. She snaps her hand free from mine and places her closed fists on her hips. Her lips tighten as she glares at me. "I don't now—nor have I *ever*—needed a man to pay for my damn coffee. I will pay for my own shit. I don't care if you've got more money than Trump. I can pay for my own bloody coffee."

I smile down at her. Everyone else in the café has gone eerily quiet. Some have already made a hasty escape towards the exit. Speaking of infinitives, *no one* talks to me like this. *Ever.*

I lean into her space. Holding her face in both of my palms, I tilt it upwards and slam my lips down hard on hers. Her gasp gives me the entrance my tongue was hoping for, as it swirls around inside her mouth. I get my first taste of her. And instantly, I know this woman could very well be my downfall. All it took was: three heartbeats, two seconds, and one taste. And I was hers.

I know I'll do anything to keep this forever. Once her shock wears off, she returns the kiss with fervor. Her arms wrap around my neck, pulling me closer. *Tighter.* Little does she know... her efforts are pointless. Because I'm never letting go.

My hands move backwards, tangling in the long, soft strands of her hair. Her vanilla scent fills my nostrils, the soft curves of her body a distinct contrast to the hard ridges of mine, as she presses up against me. I slowly pull away, resisting everything the rest of me is screaming out to do. If I don't stop now, I'll end up having her sprawled across a table. Spread out in front of me.

Leaning in, I whisper in her ear, "If it really means that much to you, I'll give you my banking information and you can pay me back. However, you can never do so upfront. Especially not here. It's something I can't explain just yet... but in our family, I have to pay for my woman."

Holly shakes her head, like she's trying to clear her thoughts. "Well, I'll agree to those terms—at the moment—and pay you back every penny. But me *being your woman* is awfully presumptuous of you. We haven't even had a first date yet."

"You are my woman; you just haven't accepted it yet. Now, should we start our day and the beginning of our second definitely not-a-date?" I take hold of her hand again and lead her out of the café.

Loui, my driver, is waiting at the sidewalk. He opens the back passenger door as we approach the car. "Morning, boss."

"Morning, you get the list I sent?"

"Sure did. I've got Sammy and Jonny scouting out the shops ahead of us."

"Great." I wait for Holly to jump in the back seat before I lean in to Loui. "If anything goes down today, get her the fuck out. That's an order."

Loui doesn't let his shock show outwardly, but the tiny flicker in his eyes tells me it's there all the same. "Ah, sure thing, boss. Are we expecting trouble?"

"Always." I smirk. We're the fucking mafia; there's always trouble *and* people looking to start it. I'm also not usually out in public during daylight hours, so my vigilance is heightened.

I'm a little on edge during the car ride to the first

store. Holding Holly's hand in mine, I rest it on my thigh. My thumb absentmindedly circles her wrist.

"Are you sure you want to be doing this? I really don't mind going alone."

"I'm certain there is nothing else I'd rather be doing." I turn and look her up and down. She's fully covered in a pair of jeans and a big coat—*I'd love to get her out of those clothes.* "Well, maybe there is one thing I'd rather be doing, but considering this is only our second not-a-date, I think I'll wait until at least the third."

"At least, huh?" she says as a blush runs up her cheeks.

The car pulls up to the curb outside the first store. I reach over and stop Holly from exiting—like she was about to. "Always wait for the door to be opened *for you.*" I can tell by her expression she doesn't like that idea. *At all.* "Please. I know it probably seems odd, or pointless, but trust me on this. I need you to always wait for Loui to open your door. It's his job, a job he takes very seriously, and it would be hard for him to do his job if you don't wait."

I decide to leave out the part about it being for her own safety—the delay gives Loui time to check our surroundings before she exits. The whole car is bullet-proof and tinted. No one can see that she's inside, but they most certainly fucking know I'd be.

I won't have her harmed in the crossfire. Fuck, maybe this was a bad idea, bringing her out. If she had gone by herself, no one would know she's important to me. No one would see us together and realize she's my one weakness—one I swore I'd never have.

"Okay, but just so we're on the same page, I'm more than capable of opening my own doors." She smiles.

Seeing her face light up releases some of the tension in my shoulders. I can't help myself. I lean in and lay a gentle kiss on her lips. "Thank you," I whisper as the door opens. I climb out and scan up and down the street, before turning back into the car and offering her my hand.

"You know, you have this whole gentleman routine down pat. Your mother must have taught you well."

"I'm sure she'll be pleased to hear that. You should tell her when you meet her." I smirk, knowing that my mother would love nothing more than to hear what a great job she's done raising me.

Holly coughs before nodding her head. "Sure, but let's save that for our fiftieth non-date, shall we?"

"Maybe. We'll see."

Shopping with Holly wasn't as easy as I thought it would be. We're at store number five. Over the last four hours, she's gone around and around the same five stops on her list. She's made a few purchases, but they haven't progressed easily.

I don't think I've ever met someone so indecisive when it comes to choosing furniture. I don't complain though. I'm obsessed with learning every little thing there is to know about her, locking every tiny facial expression away in my memory.

Who would have thought her contemplative look would be so damn captivating? She's fucking stunning. I've scowled at more men than I can count, urging them not-so-subtly to avert their fucking eyes.

"Mr. Valentino, it's great to see you. What brings you in today?" Calli smiles brightly at me from the counter. Her overly painted red lips turn down slightly when she spots my gorgeous companion.

I know Calli very well. We went to school together; her family *associates* with mine. Why didn't I remember she fucking owned this furniture shop? "I'm helping a friend out. Holly's just moved here; she's furnishing a whole apartment."

"Oh. That's great. Also, I hear congratulations are in order. You and Lana finally set a wedding date. And on Valentine's Day of all days—it's so romantic, T," Calli says wistfully.

Fuck. This is not going to bode well for me. I see it before I even turn. Hear it before the contact is even made. The hand that comes and strikes me right across the face. I could have blocked it, but I didn't.

"Holly, wait. It's not what you think." Fuck, even I know I sound fucking lame.

"What I think... is that you're engaged, Theo. Tell me it's not true?" she pleads.

"I am, but it's not in the way you're suggesting." I look around and see we're causing quite the spectacle in the middle of a public place. "Come with me. Let me explain."

"Explain? No need. I understand quite perfectly. I honestly thought you were different... special." She shakes her head and spins on her heel.

Fuck, I cannot let her walk away from me like this.

Chapter Ten

Holly

I can't believe I let myself fall into this false sense of security with Theo. Honestly, deep down in my soul, I thought he was different. Why does my heart feel like it just shattered?

I've only known this man for two bloody days. It shouldn't hurt this bad. It's never hurt like this before. I don't get it. I don't *like* it.

I turn and walk away. I need to get out of this shop

before I fall apart in front of everyone. I need to get back to my apartment.

My whole body is suddenly lifted off the ground. I don't even have time to think before I'm thrown over a broad shoulder. *Fat lot of good Bray's self-defense techniques have done me.*

"Stop! Put me down before I scream bloody murder," I seethe.

"I'm never letting you walk away from me, Holly. Scream all you like; no one will do a damn thing to stop me."

I wiggle as much as I can, hit and kick my legs, all while screaming my lungs out. But he's right; no one does a thing to help me. I'm thrown into the back seat of the car again, and Theo quickly climbs in before slamming the door shut.

"Loui take us to my apartment," Theo grunts out.

"No, Loui, let me the fuck out of here." I try the door handles—and of course they don't bloody open.

"I told you: I'm not letting you go. I need to explain things to you, but I can't do that here."

"And I told *you*: I don't need you to explain. I understand how engagements and marriages work, Theo. I'm not a bloody idiot."

"No, you're not. But you don't understand how those things work in *my* world. I just need an hour—give me an hour to show you."

"Why? Tell me why I should waste any more of my time with you?"

"Because I know I'm not the only one who feels this thing between us. I know you feel it too, Holly. This, us, we're different. Please don't give up on us before we've even had a chance to begin... I'm begging you. And I don't fucking beg anyone."

Well, damn, his words sure are pretty. But can I really take the risk and let him talk me around? What are his plans? To have me be the other woman in his life? *That* will never happen. No matter how many pretty words he throws my way.

But what have I really got to lose by hearing him out? I give a slight nod, and I see him visibly exhale. "Okay, but I'm never going to be the other woman, Theo. If that's your plan here, it's not happening."

"I promise *you* are the *only* woman." He picks up my hand, threading our fingers together. I should pull away. I should tell him where to shove his excuses and what not, but I just can't seem to let go.

He's right: we are different. Whatever this is between us, it's different from anything I've ever felt. It has to be the real thing. I have to believe he has a perfectly rational explanation for having a fiancée.

Even thinking it makes me want to hurl. I can't stop the tears before a few strays fall down my face. Theo's hand comes up and wipes my cheek.

"Odio vedere le tue lacrime. Sei troppo bella per essere i così triste," Theo whispers. I have no idea what he's just said, but it sounds beautiful. Not to mention, the tingles his words elicit, in regions that have no business tingling right now.

"What does that mean?" I ask.

"I said: I hate to see your tears. You are far too beautiful to be so sad."

"And you are far too smooth for my heart to handle."

"I will not break your heart, dolcezza. I promise you that."

"You can't know that."

"And yet I do." Theo pulls out his phone and dials a number. I can hear the call connect, and after a few short rings, a female voice answers. "L, I need you to meet me at my apartment—*now*." I can't make out what's being said on the other end. I do, however, put two and two together and gather he's speaking to his fiancée. I attempt to tug my hand away from Theo's. He just glances down with a scowl and holds on tighter. "No, now, Lana. It's important." Again, I don't catch her response. "Because I fucking asked you to. If you don't, I might have to give your daddy a call and drop the name of that Russian boyfriend you think no one knows about." A pause. "Like I said, it's fucking important. Be there in twenty." Theo hangs up the phone.

I shift my head and look out the window. I'm not sure how to take his ruthlessness. He's so full-on and demanding. It scares me, yet I'm also turned on. Shit, I'm in way over my head here.

My phone rings. Bending down, I swipe my purse from the floor. Theo reluctantly lets go of my hand so I can answer. Although, by the time I shuffle through the contents of my bag, I've missed the call. I know it's Reilly, and she's just going to call straight back. And she does. Within seconds, my phone starts up again— but this time, it's a video chat.

I answer it, holding the screen away from Theo so she can't see him. "Hey, Rye, what's up?" I try my fake happy voice. If only it would work on her...

"Cut the bullshit, Holly. Why are you crying? And why do I have a sudden sharp pain in my chest? What happened?"

"Argh, nothing happened. It's allergies—I have allergies and was running errands. I got a stitch. Maybe you got a stitch too?" I suggest.

"You're a shitty fucking liar, Hol. Try again," Reilly says, to which Theo chuckles.

"Hold up, what was that? *Who* was that? Holly, rotate the phone all the way around, nice and slowly. Actually, wait! Let me get Bray." Reilly yells out to her husband, and he shouts something back.

"Rye, stop. Look, there is no one here other than me and the Uber driver." I turn the phone around so she can see Loui in the front seat, hoping I'll get away without introducing her to Theo—you know, more formally this time.

But I'm not so lucky... He snatches the phone right out of my hands and turns the camera on himself. "And me, I'm Theo. It's nice to meet you, Reilly. I've heard a lot about you."

"Well, unfortunately, I can't say the same thing about you. Why are you with my sister, and why is she fucking sad?" Reilly asks.

"Stop." I go for the phone, but Theo holds it out of my reach.

"I'm with your sister because she's fucking amazing. And she's sad because we had a little... *misunderstanding*. But I'm working on fixing that as we speak."

"Just so you know, if you hurt my sister, I will find you. I will chop you up into tiny pieces and feed you to the great whites. I'm not afraid to get my hands dirty, and I know how to fight."

"Who are you threatening now, babe?" Bray's voice comes through louder.

"Okay, that's enough." I jump up and grab the phone. "Rye, I'm going to call you back later."

"Don't you dare hang up. Bray, she's with a man," Reilly yells out.

Bray's face fills the screen. "Hol, you doing okay? Your sister is driving me fucking nuts here. You know, if you want, I can have a jet fueled and ready for you to come home—just say the word."

Theo's head snaps towards me and the phone. I shake my head at him. "I'm fine, Bray. Reilly is just crazy, but you already knew that before you married her, so more fool you, really." I laugh.

"Yeah, but she's my kind of crazy. I love it. So, who's the guy? Does he have a name?" Bray questions.

"You know, I never actually got his name. I'll be sure to ask him next time I see him though. Gotta go! Chat later. Love you both." I hang up the phone and return it to my bag. Turning, I see Theo is still scowling. I'm reminded of when Reilly and I were kids, and how our nana warned us that our faces would freeze like that if we held the expressions for too long. I laugh a little.

"Something amusing?" Theo grunts.

"Just something my nana used to say. What's wrong with you anyway?"

"Nothing. We're here. Just so you know, if you try to run, I will catch you."

"And just so you know, your threats don't scare me."

"Well, then you'd be the first."

Chapter Eleven

Fuck! *Fuck! Fuck!* My internal thoughts consist of that one fucking word. I really fucking hope like hell I can fix this. I need to get Holly to understand the engagement between me and Lana is not real. But how the fuck do I do that without telling her I'm the fucking underboss of one of the five families? She's smart. Too fucking smart to stick around. To settle down with a made man.

She doesn't deserve to be brought into this fucked-up world. She's far too innocent. *But fuck it.* I'm selfish, and I'm keeping her for as long as I possibly can.

She's not afraid of my threats—I almost laughed when she said that. Everyone's afraid of me, everyone except this fiery redhead with an attitude far larger than her petite frame would suggest. I wonder if she'd feel the same way if she knew just what I was capable of doing. What I *have done* all my life.

I sure fucking hope so. The last thing I want is a wallflower for a wife.

Wife? I don't know where that thought came from, but I like it. *That* could be my way out of this bullshit with Lana. If I'm already married, I can't very well marry someone else. And divorce is not an option in our family. Once you're in, you're in for life. Shit... I'd be signing Holly's death warrant. I have no doubts when it comes to what lengths either of our fathers would go to, in order to get what they wanted. She'd have a hit out on her in no time.

My hand tightens around Holly's. I'm looking around the entire lobby as we make our way to the elevators.

"What's wrong? And don't bother saying nothing. I can tell something is off."

"A lot of things are *off* right now, Holly," I reply, leading her into the elevator.

"Okay, how about you start with one thing? Maybe I can help?"

I look over her features. She's genuinely worried about me. I'm surprised and not really sure how to proceed. Other than a handful of people, I can't say I've ever had anyone actually concerned about my welfare—just the ramifications should they fail to do their jobs. "Well, you could promise that you won't leave me. You walking away is my biggest fear right now."

"I-I can't promise that, Theo."

"I know. Then promise me this." I push her up against the mirrored wall. My hand brushes her hair behind her ear. "Promise that no matter what you hear about me, you'll always come to me and ask me for the truth. Promise that you'll always believe me when I say I would never hurt you, Holly. I would take a bullet for you, and slaughter the fuck out of anyone who tries to harm a single hair on your head. But... I will never hurt you."

Her eyebrows draw down. "It's hard to think when you're so close. You make my mind go fuzzy."

"You don't need to think, dolcezza, just feel. Feel this thing between us; it's the real deal."

"I do feel it, and it's scaring the shit out of me, Theo. I don't even know you, yet the thought of losing it—losing you—is suffocating me." I lean in, to kiss away her hesitation, but she turns her head and my mouth lands on her cheek instead. "I can't kiss you while you're engaged to someone else. You're not mine to kiss, Theo."

"I'm not marrying Lana. I've never belonged to anyone until you, Holly. Trust me when I say you have all of me."

"Yet you're engaged to someone else. I'm not about to be a homewrecker and break some poor girl's heart by stealing her fiancé. No matter how much I want to keep you. I'm not that cruel."

I laugh—out loud—a full-bellied laugh. "You're not a homewrecker. You'll see: the last thing Lana wants is to marry me." The doors open into my penthouse. "Come on, let me get you a drink. What would you like?"

"Just water's fine," Holly says as she looks around the open floor plan. Most people are impressed by the opulence, by the views and sheer expense. Holly doesn't look the least bit moved.

She's so... unique. And I feel like I'm way out of my depth here.

***

Fifteen minutes later, Lana walks into my penthouse. She's not alone though...

"What'd you bring him for?" I ask, nodding my head towards Neo.

"So someone could stop your crazy ass—you know, if my untimely death is your solution to this fucked-up marriage," Lana replies.

Holly, who is sitting next to me, stiffens and tries to

shift farther away. I take hold of her hand to keep her where she should be—*right fucking next to me.*

"I'm honored you think I could stop him if he wanted you dead." Neo laughs before taking a seat on the sofa opposite us. "Hi, I'm Neo, and you are absolutely fucking stunning, obviously." He reaches out a hand to Holly.

She tentatively returns the gesture. "I'm Holly. Nice to meet you." I snatch her arm back before Neo can grab hold of her open palm.

"*You*, I wouldn't think twice about shooting," I warn my cousin, who just laughs in response.

"Well, Holly, it seems you have our boy all twisted up here. What's going on?" Neo directs his question to me.

"I need Lana to explain to Holly that there is no way in hell we're actually getting married."

"Oh, don't worry, babe, I'd slit my own wrists before I'd allow myself to be any part of that hellish union. Trust me when I say: I have absolutely no intention of marrying him, now or ever." Lana visibly shudders as she sits next to Neo.

"I don't understand... Why are you engaged if neither of you intend on getting married?"

"It's a family thing. An arranged marriage, organized by our idiot fathers," Lana answers.

"Well, can't you just tell them no?" Neo and Lana chuckle at Holly's question. She doesn't understand how our world works.

"Nobody tells the boss *no*," Neo says. Fuck, I don't want to have to explain the whole mafia thing to Holly right now... on top of this marriage bullshit.

"Ah, it's a little more complicated than that. I'm working on a way out. I just need you to give me some time."

"Okay."

"Okay? You'll give me time to fix this."

Holly stands. "Take all the time you need, Theo. While you're doing that, I'll be living my *new* life in my *new* apartment. Who knows? I might even run into some dashing young stranger—who's not already engaged to someone else." My blood boils at her words. Like fuck is she going to date some other guy. "It was nice meeting you both. I'm sorry if I seem rude or whatever, but I really do need to get home."

"Wait." Shit, I can't let her leave. I can't. I jump to my feet and take her hand, dragging her down the hallway to my bedroom before slamming the door shut behind us. "Don't go. Please, just stay." I press my body against hers, leaning into the wall.

"Theo, I need space. I need to go home." Her hands land on my chest, pushing slightly.

"Okay, I'll let you go home. But, Holly, I *need* you to know that you're mine. There will be no other man."

"That's what you're worried about? Theo, you have a fucking fiancée."

"Not in the typical sense. I've never so much as touched Lana, and I don't ever intend to."

"Why not? She's beautiful."

"She's like a fucking sister. I've known her since we were toddlers. It's not happening. You and me, that's what's happening."

"I need to go home," she repeats.

I take a breath in. Against all my instincts, I know I have to let her leave. I can't start our life together by locking her in my penthouse as a prisoner. "Let me get Loui to bring the car around. I'll drop you off."

"No need. I'll get an Uber."

"You're not getting an Uber. I'll drive you." I take a step back and hold the door open. Returning to the living area—and to Lana and Neo's bickering *as per usual*—I clear my throat. "I'm giving Holly a ride home. You two can see yourselves out."

Lana stands, shocking us both as she approaches and throws her arms around Holly. "I'm so glad Theo found you. Give him a chance; he's not so bad once you get to know him."

Holly's eyebrows draw down. "Didn't you just say you'd slit your wrists before you'd marry him?"

"Well, yeah, because eww. I mean, that's just gross. It'd be like incest or something."

"Thank you," Holly says. I can tell she's not feeling all that comfortable. I need to get her out of here.

"Come on, let's go." I lead her to the elevator and wait for the doors to close before asking, "What are you thinking right now?"

"I'm thinking... I... I'm so bloody confused I don't know what to think."

"What are you confused about?"

"Everything. You. Why I feel like this. I don't even know you. Why your family is arranging marriages in the twenty-first century? The list is endless, really."

"My family has traditions that extend way back. The kind that won't ever go away."

"You act like your family's the mafia, Theo. What's really going to happen if you say no to this engagement?"

Fuck, I can't answer that. I don't want to lie to her, but I don't want to tell her the truth either. The doors open to the garage, and I walk us over to the blacked-out Lamborghini.

Holly gets into the passenger's side. She's silently watching me, dissecting my every move. It's not until we're out on the road that she asks again, "Theo, tell me your family isn't the bloody mafia. What's going to happen if you say no to this engagement?"

"I can't tell you that, dolcezza."

"That you're not in the mafia, or the part about what will happen?"

"If I say no, it will either start a war, or end with a bullet between my eyes."

"Just my bloody luck. Move to New York, Holly. It'll be a *great* place to start over," she mumbles to herself.

"Holly, I will find a way out of this marriage. You and I will get our chance."

"I'm sorry, but you're the fucking mafia, Theo. I'm not stupid, and you just said you either have to start a war, or end up dead. And both are options I'm very fucking opposed to. I think it's best if we just call it what it is: we're not going to work out."

"I'm not giving you up, Holly."

"You don't have a choice, Theo. You have to."

"There's always a choice, and I fucking choose you. I choose us."

Chapter Twelve

Holly

I *fucking choose you.* Theo's words run wild through my head. I'm not sure if he was intending to mess me up the way he has or not. But, either way, I'm more conflicted now than I was before. I'd love to believe his pretty words. In my heart, I do believe them. In my head, however, I'm telling myself not to be so bloody naïve. To run while I still can. I should take Bray up on that offer to have a jet ready for me to fly home. That would be the smart thing to do.

Instead, I let Theo escort me down the hallway. I turn the key in the lock and open the door, placing a hand on his chest to stop him from following me inside. I can't let him come in. I have to distance myself from him, to clear my head and come to my senses. "I need you to give me time and space."

"Why?"

"Because in my head, I'm messed up. I need to process things. Alone."

"You're not alone in this, Holly. We are in this thing together. You don't have to process anything alone."

"I just... I can't right now. I'm sorry." I close the door and lock it, remembering to slide the chain in place too.

I'm so bloody exhausted, both physically and mentally. All I want to do is curl up in bed. I head for a shower. And as soon as I'm under the water, I let the tears fall. I'm so frustrated right now. I can't do this. I can't handle the ache that's forming in my heart. It makes absolutely no sense. I don't know anything about this man other than his name's Theo, and he apparently has an arranged fiancée who he's refusing to marry. Oh, yeah, and he's in the bloody mafia.

That last part alone should have me running for the hills. I'm a good person. I have morals. What kind of hypocrite would I be if I backpedaled on those beliefs now, all for a pretty face and a well-defined body?

But, boy, is it one well-defined body... I remember having him pressed against me when he kissed me in the café like no one was watching. I wanted nothing more than to jump his bones. It's odd to think that *that* moment was only hours ago. It feels like so much has happened since then. None of it good.

I choose you. His voice haunts me. I can't seem to get those three words out of my mind. Has anyone ever chosen me before? I don't know, but I don't think so... not anyone that I can recall anyway.

I get out of the shower, then put on an old sweat-shirt and fluffy socks. Curling up under the blankets in bed, I call the one person who will never judge me. It's three in the morning in Sydney, but I need her.

"Holly? Is everything okay?" Reilly's sleepy voice answers.

"No. I don't know."

"Hold on, let me move so we don't wake the beast."

"Too late. What's wrong?" Bray asks from beside her.

"It's a sister thing. Go back to sleep, babe." Reilly gets out of bed and exits the bedroom. I wait for her to settle herself in the kitchen. "Okay, what's going on?"

"How did you know Bray was the one? How soon did you honestly know he was different from other guys?"

"This is about a man... A guy has you so worked up

that you're calling me at three a.m. Well, he must be something else." Reilly smiles.

"Shut up. I shouldn't have called. Forget I asked."

"Wait, okay. I knew Bray was different the very first time I saw him. Although, you and I both know I tried to run like hell and get as far away from those feelings as I could."

"*How* did you know?"

"I could feel his presence in a room before I even saw him. There was obviously an indescribable chemistry between us that I'd never felt before. I mean, the man has one hell of a magical cucumber."

"Reilly, focus. I don't need to hear about his pierced cucumber."

"Right, sorry. It's just very distracting. Anyway, I knew because when I thought of being without him, my heart hurt. Just like I know yours is right now. What happened?"

"You wouldn't believe me if I told you. It's just crazy... I've only known T for two days, but I feel this weird connection I've never felt before. It's different from our twin thing."

"So, why are you fighting it? Is it a limp dick or something?"

"No, well, actually... I don't know but I doubt it. He kissed me today, and I could feel that kiss everywhere."

"Again, what's wrong then?"

"I don't know if I should trust him. If I should let

myself be vulnerable to him breaking my heart. If I feel this bad after two days, how will I feel if in a week or a month, he changes his mind and finds someone better?"

"You are Holly fucking Reynolds. There is no one better than you. If he breaks your heart, I'll break his stupidly handsome face."

"It *is* stupidly handsome, isn't it? A man shouldn't be allowed to be that good looking, right?"

"Right."

"Thanks, Reilly. Go back to bed. Sorry I called at such a ridiculous time."

"Holly, you can call me at any time. I will always answer for you. If you need me, you know I'll be on the first plane over."

"I know. I love you."

"Not nearly as much as I love you, sister."

I disconnect the call and the tears fall again. I miss my twin. I miss my old life. My friends. But I can't go back to all that and wonder *what would have been.* Darkness is starting to seep into the room, and I can't seem to stop crying. I'm going to end up with ugly puffy eyes tomorrow. I need to try to get some sleep.

I've been lying in bed sobbing for what feels like hours when I hear him. I know it's him. I can smell him. I can feel him. I don't bother moving. I have the brief thought to tell him to leave. Instead, I just lie here as he climbs in behind me. He plucks me up and turns me over, wrapping his arms around me so my head is resting on his shoulder, my face buried into his chest.

"What are you doing here?" I sniffle.

"I couldn't stand to sit outside your door and listen to you cry any longer. I'm sorry, Holly. So fucking sorry."

"How'd you get in? I locked the chain." That's what I say? I literally have a shirtless Theo in my bed, and all I can think to say is: *I locked the chain?*

Wait, hold up. I have a shirtless Theo in my bed. My hands suddenly have a mind of their own, as they travel up and down the ridges of his torso. Shit, this is not good.

"Dolcezza, as much as I love you touching me, that's not what I came in here for. I want to make you feel better. Tell me how to make you feel better."

"I'm going to go to hell for this," I whisper before I confess, "I want you to touch me, Theo. I want you to kiss me again. I want everything you're promising."

"*That*, I can do." Theo smirks, slamming his mouth down hard on mine. His teeth nibble at my bottom lip until I open for him, his tongue greedily swirling around my own.

My hands continue to run up and down his body. I can't get enough. It's as if I've been set alight for the first time in my life, every nerve ending responding to his touch. I'm burning up. I need to get out of this sweater. Pulling away, I sit up and throw the material over my head. Next, I pull off my fluffy socks in a very unsexy-like movement.

I look back at Theo, who is just staring wide-eyed at me. A rush of self-consciousness seeps in, and I go to cover myself with the blanket.

Theo grabs my hands and holds them down at my sides. "Don't. I want to look at every inch of you. I want to burn this image in my memory. You are fucking gorgeous, Holly. So fucking gorgeous I don't know where to start." He lifts my arms above my head, clasping both wrists in one hand. "I could start worshiping you here." The fingers of his free hand trail down the side of my neck. "Or here," he says as his tongue swipes across my right nipple before moving on to the left.

"Mmm, there is good." My back arches off the bed, offering my breast to him.

"It's better than good; it's fucking magnificent." He releases his grip on my wrists, using both of his palms to cup my breasts as his mouth explores and devours my nipples.

He takes his time. I'm a wet, writhing mess when one of his hands finally travels down my belly, right to my clit.

"Oh, fuck." I'm so worked up I think I'm going to come. His finger rubs circles around my clit before dipping inside me. He adds another digit and pumps in and out. I feel my whole body tighten as I reach climax embarrassingly fast. "Ah, shit, fuck. Theo. Yes, there!" I ramble on.

"Holy Mother of God. I need to see it again," he says, leaning in and kissing my lips.

"See what?" I'm confused...

"You, coming apart for me. I need to see it again. And again. And again. I've never seen anything so fucking perfect."

Theo settles himself between my thighs. My legs wrap around his waist, my fingers pulling on the belt of his pants. I finally get it undone and proceed with unfastening his button and fly. I reach my hand in and free his cock from the confines of his boxers. Wrapping my palm around the firmness, I stroke it up and down, collecting the precum on my fingers each time I reach the tip.

"Fuck, Holly, if you keep doing that, I won't last another minute. And I need to be buried inside your pussy like I need air to breathe."

I remove my hand and nod my head in agreement. "Yes, that. Do that. Now," I urge him.

"Hold that thought." I wait as he retrieves a foil packet from his pocket and slips his legs out of his pants. The room is dark, the only illumination coming from the streetlight seeping in from the window. But I can make out the silhouette of his body, watching as he rolls the condom on before he lines himself up with my entrance. He looks down, hovering above me. *What is he waiting for?* I squeeze my thighs around him and draw him in. I don't need him to wait. I need to feel him inside me. *Now.* "You know this means you're mine, right? I'm never gonna be able to let you go." His voice is strained. Like he's trying to hold back.

"Then don't ever let me go." I pull his mouth down to mine. He begins to move in and out of me. Slowly. I grow even wetter as my body becomes accustomed to his size.

I meet each thrust. I need more, but how do I tell him I want it harder? Faster? I've never been comfortable with sex. I've had it—obviously—but I've always been on the shy side, just going along for the ride. It's been enjoyable, but I've never had the guts to ask for what I want.

As I'm contemplating this in my head, Theo stops thrusting and flips us over so that now I'm straddling him. I can feel him even deeper this way.

"I want you to take everything you need. Show me what you want." I don't think he understands what he's asking of me. I can't be in control like this. I don't know how. "Don't overthink it, Holly. Do whatever makes you feel good. Put my hands where you want them. Move in a way that feels good to you."

"But what about what you want?"

"What I want is for you to enjoy this, because I plan on doing this again. So, don't worry about me. Trust me when I say being buried balls deep in you feels better than anything I've ever felt before."

I close my eyes and start to move my hips back and

forward. His hands slide up my waist and stop just before they reach my chest. I place my open palms on top of his and guide them up so they are cupping my breasts. He doesn't need any more of a hint; he starts pinching and twisting at my nipples. My body arches and my hips move faster, my pelvis grinding down on his. I can feel the tingles all through my body. It's so intense. I'm chasing a release I just can't seem to catch. I'm about to give up when his hand dips lower. He pinches my clit, and that little twinge of pleasure-pain sends me soaring over the cliff.

When I come to, Theo is smiling up at me. "Fucking perfect. So fucking beautiful." At this moment, I'm thankful for the darkness we're cloaked in because I can feel the blush warming my cheeks. "Now it's my turn. If at any stage it gets to be too much or too rough, tell me and I'll stop, okay?" I'm confused. Why would I tell him to stop? But before I can ask the question, I'm flipped onto my back. One of my legs goes up and rests on Theo's shoulder, while he wraps the other around his waist. "You might want to brace yourself, dolcezza." That's the only warning I get before he starts thrusting into me. Hard and fast.

Yes, this is how I imagined a guy like Theo would take me. Who needs soft and gentle when you can have... *this*?

Theo doesn't give up, even as I clench down on him in the midst of my third orgasm of the night. He's like the bloody Energizer Bunny and I freaking love it.

My voice is sore from the amount of screaming I've done. I wouldn't be surprised if the whole apartment complex knew that Theo was in here laying claim to my vagina. And what a good bloody job he is doing.

I'm officially fucked. *Both literally and metaphorically.* Because as his thrusts become rigid and he stills on top of me—my name on his lips like a prayer—I know I'm never going to be able to give this man up.

Come hell or high water, Theo Valentino is mine.

Chapter Thirteen

I wake with a jolt when I hear a scream. Bolting upright, I grab the handgun I tucked under the bed last night before I climbed in beside Holly.

"Ah, fuck, what the fuck was that for?" The voice is muffled.

"Why are you in my apartment, and how the bloody hell did you get in?" Holly screams again.

I run out into the empty space of Holly's living

room, gun aimed. *I should take out a kneecap just to teach the son of a bitch a lesson.*

"Sorry... T texted saying you needed new locks. Don't shoot the messenger." Neo holds up a bag from the hardware store.

I lower the gun to my side, seeing as the only threat here is my dipshit cousin. "Thanks," I say, reaching for the bag.

"You okay, Holly? You're looking a little pale?" Neo questions.

Fuck... Glancing over to Holly, I note that her eyes are hyper-focused on the gun in my hand, and her skin has blanched. "Dolcezza, what's wrong?" She doesn't answer. However, she does faint. Neo catches her before her body hits the ground. I drop both the bag and the gun, having her out of his arms in less than five seconds. "What the fuck did you do to her?" I yell as I carry her back into the bedroom.

Neo follows. "Not a thing, I swear, T. I just got here, and she kicked me in the balls."

"Holly, wake up." I lay her down on the bed and hold her head in my hands. *What the fuck do I do?* "I swear to God: I will fucking kill you if you touched her, Neo." I know my anger is misplaced. There is no one else on this earth I'd trust Holly's safety with, and I know my cousin wouldn't harm her in any way.

"I'd let you. But I swear she looked fine until you came running out."

"Fuck, Holly, wake up," I yell a little louder, and her eyes flutter open.

"What happened?" she says, trying to sit up.

I push her back down. "Don't move. You fainted. Neo, get the doc here."

"Neo, stop. I don't need a doctor. I'm fine," Holly insists, pushing at my hands.

"You're not fine; you just passed out."

"I'm fine. I..." She looks towards the doorway and, noticing the audience, stops her sentence.

"Neo, wait for the doc at the front door."

"Yeah, okay. Are you sure you're all right, Holly? I'm really sorry if I did anything to make you pass out," he says before stepping over the threshold.

"You didn't. Don't worry about it." She smiles shyly at him as he turns the corner. Once he's gone, Holly covers her face with her hands and her body sags against the headboard. "I'm so sorry. I'm so embarrassed."

"You don't need to be sorry or embarrassed. I just need to know what happened. I need to fix this. Does this happen often? You fainting?" Fuck, if she has a habit of fainting, I'm never going to be able to leave her side. What if she's walking down a flight of stairs and passes out? Shit, what if she's on the sidewalk and falls?

"No, only when I'm overcome with fear..."

"Neo scared you so much you fainted?" I ask, ready to actually go and put that bullet in his kneecap.

"No, you did," she whispers. Her words cut deep. So fucking deep.

I scared her? "What? I don't...? What did I do? I'm sorry—the last thing I want to do is scare you." I pull her onto my lap, my hands stroking through the long strands of her hair.

"It wasn't you, necessarily; it was the gun. I don't like them. I don't like seeing them."

"The gun? I'd never aim a gun at you."

"I just... There was an incident... back home. There was this guy, and he-he—" Her breathing begins to pick up faster.

"Holly, relax, you're safe here. You are safe with me." I haven't even heard her story, and I'm already calculating how long it will take me to have a jet ready to fly out to Sydney.

"He, um, he was in the club and I walked in. I was meant to be meeting Reilly, and he was there. He thought I was her... He wanted to hurt Bray and mistook me for my sister."

I rub my hands up and down her back. I'm not sure if I'm trying to calm her *or myself* at this point. "What did he do, Holly?" My voice is hoarse.

"He pointed the gun at me. I really thought he was going to shoot. Then I heard the gunfire. He shot Bray right in front of us all—*my brother-in-law was in a coma for two months*. I had to watch my sister, my twin sister, have her heart break each day he didn't wake up."

"I'm sorry you experienced that. What happened to the shooter?" I ask, purely for selfish reasons.

"I don't know. Zac just told me I didn't need to worry, that the guy wouldn't ever be seen again. I didn't ask questions."

Who the fuck are these guys Holly was hanging around with back in Sydney? "Who's Zac?" I pry, letting my agitation and jealousy creep out.

Holly smiles. "Zac is—well, he owns the hottest nightclub in Sydney. Oh, and he's also *hot*. Like GQ hot." She laughs at my obvious distress. "Aside from his looks, he's Bray's brother and my good friend Alyssa's husband."

"You couldn't have led with that?" I ask her as my body loosens slightly.

"I could have, but it wouldn't have been anywhere near as fun. I'm going to go have a shower. You can finish making coffee and tell Neo I don't need a doctor."

"Deal, but I'd much rather be joining you in the shower." My mouth travels up the side of her neck.

"Mmm, that would be fun. But, no, sorry. You invited your cousin to my apartment, so you entertain him."

"I can tell him to leave," I suggest.

"That would be rude." Her lips mimic mine and travel up the side of my neck until she gets to the corner of my mouth.

"It's Neo; he's used to me ordering him around."

"Anyone ever tell you that you're really good at negotiations?"

"I run multi-million-dollar companies; it comes with the territory."

Holly's head pulls back and her eyebrows draw down in confusion. "What do you mean you run companies?"

"Don't be so shocked. It's the modern age. The mafia isn't just a bunch of thugs anymore."

"I didn't think you were a thug. Well, not entirely. I guess I didn't really put much thought into what you actually do."

"Good, don't overthink it. It's a family business— one I was born into and one I'll die in. It's the way it is. I can't change that."

"You couldn't leave?"

"Never."

"Okay. I'm going for that shower." Holly jumps up and walks out of the room with a look in her eyes I can't decipher.

I stand at the bathroom door and listen for a while, making sure she hasn't fainted again. I can hear her rummaging around and then the water starting. I decide to go and find Neo. Though, considering the size of Holly's apartment, it doesn't take me long to track him down on the balcony with a cigarette in his mouth.

"She okay?" he asks as I slide the door closed behind me.

"Yeah, I think so."

"What happened?"

"She's afraid of guns. An incident occurred at some nightclub not that long ago."

"So, who do we need to make disappear?"

"No one. Apparently, it's been dealt with. Find out everything you can about the Williamson brothers in Sydney."

"Who are they?"

"One of them is Holly's brother-in-law, the other owns *that* nightclub."

"Sure. What are you going to do about her fear of guns? We can't have her passing out every time she sees one."

"I'll fix it. Speaking of, where'd mine go?" I ask. It wasn't on the floor where I left it. Neo pulls my piece from his waistband and hands it over. I tuck it into the back of my pants.

"All right, I'm out. Got shit to do. You any closer to figuring out what the fuck your pops and John are up to yet?"

"Nope. But I'm suddenly very determined to put this shit to bed."

"I bet you are," he says as he walks back through the apartment.

I follow him in and look around. I wonder if I can convince Holly to come stay at my place with me. Because I sure as fuck won't be spending another night in bed without her.

"Where are we going?" Holly asks.

"Don't freak out. But we need to get you accustomed to guns, babe. You can't pass out every time you see one. So, I'm gonna teach you how to use one."

Holly's face pales. "No, Theo, I can't. Please don't make me do this."

"Do you trust me?"

"Probably more than I should, considering I just found out yesterday you're betrothed to someone else." She smirks.

"Funny. But I'm glad to hear you say that. Now, I just need you to trust me when I promise I won't ever let anything happen to you."

"It's not that I don't trust you. I don't trust myself. And I don't trust my fear, nor its ability to override everything I know logically."

"I'll be there every step of the way. You can do this. We can do this together. I might not be able to conquer these demons for you, but I'll be right by your side when you conquer them yourself."

"What if I pass out again?"

"Then I'll catch you, and we will try and try again until you've mastered it."

"You have way more confidence in my abilities than I do," she says, looking down.

"I have confidence in *us*. There is nothing this world will ever throw at us that we can't beat together."

"Mmm, does one of those multi-million-dollar companies you run happen to be Hallmark?"

"No, why?"

"Because you'd make a bloody mint writing greeting cards with those lines of yours."

"They're not lines, just our truth."

Chapter Fourteen

Holly

Our truth? Is he for real? We barely know each other, and he's so insistent on everything being an *us*. *Together*. But then again, who am I to argue if this god of a man wants to be an *us* with me?

It's during times like these I wonder if my brother

is looking out for me. Do our deceased loved ones really guide us from above? It's a nice notion, but I'm not convinced. For years, I've asked Dylan to send me a sign that he's still with us. Just something that tells me he's not gone forever. I must be cynical... because I've yet to see a thing. Reilly says she does, and I believe that she *believes* she does. I just haven't witnessed it firsthand.

"If you are up there, Dyl, please help me find the strength to get through this. For the love of everything, do not let me pass out again," I offer the silent prayer in my head as I wait for Theo to open my door. "Thank you," I say, as I take his extended palm and he gently tugs me forward.

"Anytime." He winks at me, and I just about melt into a puddle right here in the car park of this—well, whatever *this* is.

"Ah, where are we?" I scan our surroundings. The whole area looks shady as hell. Deserted. There's one old warehouse-type building directly in front of us, flanked by similar-looking structures. We didn't drive that far so I know we are still somewhat close to the city, yet everything looks as if it hasn't seen life for centuries.

"I own the place. Don't worry, no one's around." Theo places his hand on my lower back and guides me into the building.

"I don't know how else to put it, but this place is creepy as hell, Theo. I feel like I'm the stupid girl in every horror film—the one who's placing all her trust in the serial killer leading her to her untimely demise."

"You're right; you are far too trusting. Don't trust anyone you meet from my family, Holly. Other than me of course."

"Of course. What about Neo? You seem close with him."

"I trust him with my life. If something were to happen to me and I wasn't around, he's the one you need to find. He'll take care of you."

"I don't need anyone to take care of me. And what the hell do you think is going to happen to you?" I'm getting worked up over the mere idea of something happening to him. Oh God, I didn't think this through. What *was* I thinking? I can't date a mobster, a mafia man. I don't have it in me to be that strong. I know my limits, and this is far beyond them.

Why couldn't Theo just be an ordinary banker or a lawyer even? No, I had to go fall in love with a criminal. Someone who probably does unspeakable things. Someone with lots of enemies... I've seen *The Godfather*. I know how it all works. Kind of, anyway.

Wait... love? Where did that come from? I'm not in love with him, am I?

"Have you ever been in love?" I blurt out before covering my mouth with my hands. Yep, way to have him sprinting faster than the Road Runner.

"Holly, your mind is overcomplicating things. I can literally see the wheels spinning in your eyes. Don't be afraid to ask me anything. I might not be able to answer all of your questions, but I'll do my best to give you what I can." He cups my face in his hands. "Have I been in love? I used to think the notion of love was just something they sold in movies. But now, yeah, I think I've been in love."

"Oh, okay, cool." I try to mask the hurt. He's been in love with someone else. "What happened to her?" I ask, needing to know.

"Nothing's happened to her. I'm looking at her right now."

I freeze. My mind, my body, everything freezes. He can't be serious. "This is crazy, Theo. I don't even know your favorite movie. How can we possibly be in love?"

"I don't think it's about knowing everything about one another. I think our souls *know* each other."

"Maybe." I consider what he said. It's a strange sensation: to feel something so deep for someone you barely know anything about.

"Come on. Let's make you the best shot this town has ever seen."

"I'd settle for just not passing out."

"That too." He laughs.

We've been at this for two hours. I've succeeded in not fainting. Have I hit any targets? Not a single one. But I can now hold a gun. I'm not working up a sweat. And I'm not on the brink of tears.

I still don't love these things. If I could avoid ever having to deal with them, I would. But Theo insists I know how to protect myself. That being said, I'm not sure I'm ever going to be able to aim a gun at an actual living person in order to do so.

"Holly, I want you to imagine that someone is at the other end, where that target is. They're about to shoot you. You need to save yourself, and the only way you can do that is to shoot first."

I try again. I lift the gun, aim, and fire. "Did I get it?" I ask.

"Not quite." He pauses. "Okay, let's take a break. I have another idea, but I need to get Neo out here."

Half an hour later, Neo walks into the shed with a gun in his hands. I don't freak out. *Much.* That is, until he hits Theo over the back of the head with the butt. Now I'm officially freaked the hell out. What's happening? They're both on the ground scrambling with each other.

"Fuck you, I'm going to fucking kill you, idiot," Theo roars as he punches his cousin over and over.

I back up against the wall. I don't know what to do. I have to do *something.* Theo was just telling me that Neo was the one to go to if anything were to happen to him. Why the hell are they trying to kill each other now?

Somehow, in all the chaos, Neo ends up on top while aiming the barrel directly at Theo's head. "You think you can best me? Think again, cousin." Neo spits a heap of blood onto the ground.

"Holly, get out of here—now!" Theo yells over at me. How the hell does he expect me to just leave him here? *I need to do something,* I tell myself again. I will not lose him when I only just found him.

"N-no," I say walking towards them. I see the gun I was using for practice and pick it up.

"Holly, no. Get out of here."

"You should listen to your boy, sweetheart. I won't stop at him. You know, no witnesses and all." Neo smirks.

The look that crosses Theo's face is thunderous. I'd be scared if I was on the other end of that look.

"No... I don't know why you're doing this, Neo. And I'm sorry, really sorry but I can't let you do this." I aim the gun at his chest and, without a second thought, I pull the trigger. The sound reverberates around the room, and I watch as Neo falls to the ground. I crumble right along with him.

Theo is by my side within seconds, wiping my hair away from my face. "Holly, you did it. You were fucking amazing. I fucking love you." I have ugly tears running down my face, and now's the time he chooses to say those three little words?

"I'm sorry... I don't know. I'm sorry. Shit, what have I done?"

"Damn, Holly, I didn't think you had it in you. Talk about lethal. You'll make one hell of a queen. No one will see you coming." Neo cracks his neck before sitting upright.

I jolt out of Theo's arms. The two cousins are smiling at each other like they just discovered sliced bread for the first time.

"What? What the hell?"

"Sorry, dolcezza, I had to use drastic measures to get you to overcome your fear."

"You think scaring me to death was the way to do that? To have me think you were about to die? Do you have any idea how that bloody feels, Theo?" Now I'm angry. I'm beyond angry. Fuck him and his mind games.

"Holly, you did it. Was it scary? Yes. But it worked. You picked up that gun, you shot, and you actually hit your target."

"Yeah, well, I should have bloody aimed higher. I'm not a toy with buttons you can press as you see fit. Next time you have a gun pointed at your head, save yourself. Because I won't be around to help you."

"Wait, okay, I'm sorry. I didn't mean to scare you," Theo tries to argue. I raise my eyebrows at him. *Really? Because I thought scaring me to death was exactly what he wanted.* "Okay, I did. But it was for a good reason. You were fine. I was fine. We are fine."

"You know what? You're right. I'm sorry for overre-acting. Can I have the keys to the car? I need to get my coat. It's chilly in here."

"Sure. We can get out of here if you want. Give me a minute to close up." I let him kiss my forehead as he hands me the keys.

"No, it's fine. I'll be back in a sec. I just need my coat." I take the keys and walk out as calmly as I can. Once the vehicle is within eyesight, I don't waste time getting into the driver's seat and locking the doors. I'm thankful he's another idiot who loves fast cars, because before I see Theo at the door of the building, I already have the car screeching onto the street.

I can drive. It's the one thing that usually surprises everyone, just how much I love a fast ride. I don't let up on the gas, weaving in and out of traffic. But I don't have a destination in mind. I just drive. It doesn't take too long to get the hang of the whole driving on the right side of the road thing, and soon it's like I have been doing it this way my whole life.

I can see Neo's car trailing behind me. I know he's struggling to keep up with my erratic maneuvering. I still have no idea where I'm headed. I almost lose Neo's tail over the Brooklyn Bridge. But I purposely slow down to let them catch up.

Two hours later, I follow a turn off sign that reads: Hampton Beach. A beach sounds like a good place to stop. I love the beach. I've seen more of New York in the last few hours than in the entirety of my stay. Why didn't I just rent a car and do this sooner?

I pull into a beach car park and stop the engine. I'm sitting on the bonnet of his extremely expensive car when a thunderous Theo comes storming towards me.

Shit, he looks bloody furious.

Chapter Fifteen

She stole my car. I can't believe she stole my fucking car. For over two hours, we've been struggling to keep up with her goddamn joyriding. For over two fucking hours, my heart has been at risk of exploding. I probably have fucking gray hairs. What the hell was she thinking, driving off like that? Does she have no sense of self-preservation?

I'm storming towards her—she's sitting on the

hood of my eight-hundred-thousand-dollar car. I'm fucking fuming that she took off like that. However, my relief over the fact she's in one piece and not sinking in the fucking East River is palpable.

As I get closer, her eyes search mine. She knows I'm pissed. But she's no less angry now than she was earlier either. As soon as I reach her, I pick her up and slam my lips on hers. Her legs capture my waist, and I walk around the side of the car, pressing her against the door.

Pulling away, I growl into her mouth, "Don't ever fucking scare me like that again. Do you have any idea what you just did?"

"Why were you scared? I'm a perfectly good driver. Your car doesn't even have a scratch on it."

"I wasn't worried about the fucking car, Holly. I was worried about you."

"Huh, bet that didn't feel good, now, did it?"

"Not at all." She stares at me. It takes a little while for the meaning behind her words to click. "Fuck, I'm sorry. I won't ever do anything like that again. I really was just trying to get you to overcome your fear of guns. That's all."

"I didn't like the idea that something was going to happen to you. I just found you, Theo. I'm not ready to let you go."

"Good, because I'm never going to be able to let you go." I fuse my lips with hers. I can't get enough.

"Don't ever steal my car again, Holly. If anyone else tried that, they'd be meeting a very early death."

"I'm sorry I took your car. But don't worry... I'm going to buy my own. Maybe something even faster than this thing."

"No. You should have... like a little hatchback or something. Better yet, let me give you Loui. He can drive you wherever you need to go in the SUV. It's the safest car I own."

"I'm not taking your driver. And I'm not buying a hatchback." She untangles her legs from my waist when a throat clears behind us. "How are you not dead yet?" Holly asks Neo.

"Sorry to disappoint you, sweetheart. I'm like a cat, nine lives and all."

"No, I mean, I shot you. Did I miss and you just pretended to get hit?"

"Nope, you got me right here." Neo lifts his shirt to show the bruise he's sporting.

"Oh my God, I'm so sorry. Well, actually, I'm not. Really, you bloody deserved it," Holly says as she steps closer to inspect his injury. "You should probably put some ice or something on that." Her hand reaches out to touch his chest.

And like hell am I letting that happen. I grab her around the waist and spin her around. "You know, I'm injured too. I could use some ice and someone to nurse me back to health." I point to the gash on my head, then the dried-up blood stuck to my hair.

"What the bloody hell, Theo? You should be at the hospital. You probably need stitches and a tetanus shot. Get in the car." She turns to Neo. "Why didn't you make him go to the hospital?"

"Because we were busy chasing your crazy ass down, babe."

"Holly. Her name is fucking Holly, Neo," I yell at my cousin.

"Sorry, my bad. Because we were busy chasing your crazy ass down, *Holly*!" Neo holds up his hands in surrender. "Anyway, if you're good, I'm out. It's a long trip back to the city."

"Yeah, sure, we're heading back to my place now too."

"Great. Lovely to see you as always, Holly." Neo walks to his SUV. I know he won't actually drive away until he knows we're also on the road. He's not likely to leave me out in the middle of nowhere without back-up.

"Get in." I open the passenger's side door of the car, but Holly doesn't move. She just stares at me, like she's waiting for something. "Please," I add in a softer tone.

"Was it that hard?" she asks, passing me to get inside.

"Nope." I shut the door, maybe a little more forcefully than I should. My anger over the events of the past few hours is rising again, now that the relief has dissipated.

I pull out of the car park, the wheels spinning as we turn onto the road. The next hour of the trip is silent, neither of us wanting to speak first.

Once we cross the Brooklyn Bridge, Holly breaks the tension. "Can you just drop me at my apartment? Or anywhere really. I can call for an Uber."

I look over at her. She's lost her damn mind if she thinks I'll ever drop her off to get a fucking Uber. But I'm interrupted by my phone ringing before I can respond to tell her as much. "Fuck!" I hit the steering wheel. "Whatever you hear right now, I need you to keep your mouth shut. Do not make a sound." It's the only warning I give her before I hit answer, and her glare says exactly how she feels about that. "Pops, what's happening?"

"Son, why is it that I'm hearing how you and Neo were fucking around all over the goddamn state today? What happened?"

Shit. "Nothing happened. Neo and I made a bet. That's all it was. I won, obviously."

"A bet. You drove like you were being chased down by the fucking Russians, because of a bet?"

"Yep." I keep my answers simple.

"Fucking hell, T. You need to grow the fuck up already. How do you think you'll take over this family, if you're still running around like a child?"

"I'm sure I'll manage. Besides, you have plenty of years left in you, Pops. Plenty of time for me to grow up."

"You're about to be a husband. And hopefully, not long after that, a father. You need to grow the fuck up *now*."

"Yeah, about that. Care to tell me why this marriage is so important to you?"

"All you need to know is that it is. Don't fuck this up, Theo."

"Wasn't planning on it." The phone cuts out; my father refuses to end a call with a normal gesture like *goodbye* or *talk later*. "I'm sorry," I whisper.

"For what part?" Holly asks.

"All of it. I don't know how to do this, Holly. I've never wanted to do *this* before. I need you to be patient with me. If I come across harsh or act like a dick, know that I don't mean to."

"You got the dick part right."

"Again, I'm sorry. Tell me how to fix it. What do I need to do?"

"You don't need to do anything. We've known each other for two days, Theo. You don't owe me any apologies." She turns to face me. "Drop me off at my place. Then go and get your head looked at—that really is a nasty gash. Although, I'm sure you've had worse."

"Okay," I tell her. I have to give her time. I have to give myself time. I actually have a list of shit to do if I want to find a way out of this fucking arrangement.

"Thank you."

Half an hour later, I pull up in front of her building. I park and go to get out of the car, when Holly's hand reaches over and grabs my arm.

"I don't need you to walk me up. Thank you for the ride home. I'll, um, I'll see you later." Her eyes don't meet mine. Where is the fiery woman who was just telling me and my cousin off?

Placing my fingers under her chin, I lift her face until our eyes connect. "Holly, I need you to remember one thing for me."

"What's that?"

"You are mine."

"But you're not mine, are you, Theo? You can't really be mine until you get out of whatever this marriage thing is."

"I'm yours, Holly. I will always be yours. I have some shit to do, but I'll be back later, okay?"

"Okay, I'll see you later... maybe."

I lean in and gently kiss her lips. "No, not *maybe*. You will see me later, dolcezza." I watch her walk up the stairs and don't pull away from the curb until she's inside her building.

Someone has to fucking know something. I just need to torture the information out of the right asshole. I don't care how long it takes, or how many fingers I need to break.

I down my glass of whisky. "Another." I nod to the bartender.

"Do you think that's wise? Maybe you should call it a night. I'll give you a lift home." Neo stands and drops a pile of hundreds on the bar.

"No, I gotta go to Holly's," I slur as I slide off the barstool.

"Ah, maybe you should sleep it off and go see her tomorrow."

"No, going there now." I fumble around in my pockets. "Where's my phone? I'll have Loui bring the car around."

"I've got it, and you gave Loui the night off. Let's go. I'll take you. But if she shoots me again, you're on your own."

"She saved me," I say as Neo guides me into the passenger's seat of his SUV.

"Yeah, probably in more ways than one."

I end up knocking on Holly's door. Neo is still here. Why is he still here? "You can leave now, you know," I tell him.

"Yeah, let me just make sure she doesn't kick your drunk ass to the curb first. You might need a ride home."

"She won't kick me out. She loves me. I'm very lovable, ya know."

"Since when?" he asks as I knock louder.

I'm about to bang again when the door swings open, and Holly's beautiful face comes into focus—okay, I may be seeing two of her faces and they both look mad. "You're fucking beautiful even when you're mad, dolcezza."

I lean in to kiss her, but she turns her head to the side. I stumble forward and Neo pulls me upright. He's always got my back.

"And you're drunk. What are you doing here?"

"I'm here, because you're here," I tell her. *Obviously. Because I want to be wherever she is.*

"Sorry, Holly. He insisted on me dropping him off. Want me to drag him home?" Neo asks.

"My home is Holly," I remind them. What aren't they understanding about this?

"Okay, Romeo." Holly takes my hand. I like the feel of her soft skin on mine. "Neo, help me make sure he lands on the bed, and not the floor."

"Sure. Lead the way."

I follow Holly. "Ow, fuck! When did that get there?" I don't know what I hit but it fucking hurt.

"The wall? It's always been there." Holly laughs.

"You have a beautiful laugh."

"Thanks?" She folds the blankets down, and I stumble forward as I tug my shirt over my head. I finally yank it free and throw it on the floor. I need to get out of these pants. I go for my belt but can't seem to figure it out.

"Okay, stand up." Holly pulls at my hands. "I'll

help." I do as I'm told, and her fingers go to my belt buckle.

"Wait, hold up. Let me just..." Neo walks in behind me and removes something from my waistband. "...grab this." He places my gun on the bedside table before coming back around. The room is spinning.

"Am I going to come across any more of those if I help him out of these pants?" Holly asks.

"You shouldn't, but he's likely to have a couple of knives strapped to his ankles. I'm out. My number's in his phone if you need anything, sweetheart."

"He's an asshole." I stumble as I point to my cousin.

"Why is he an asshole?" Holly works my belt free and unfastens my button and fly. She then bends down to untie the laces on my shoes.

"Fucking hell, how'd I get so lucky to find you?" Watching her on her knees is a sight to behold.

"I was hungry and your cousin has a really great café." She smirks. "Okay, step out."

I fall backwards onto the bed as I attempt to get my feet untangled from the material. Shit, the room is spinning really fast.

"Great." I hear Holly curse before the blackness takes over.

Chapter Sixteen

Holly

It's been a week since T showed up at my apartment, drunk off his arse. He returns every night. Sometimes earlier, while I'm still awake. And sometimes around two or three in the morning, when I pretend that I'm not. The truth is: I haven't actually been able to fall asleep on those nights. Not without him. I know how pathetically stupid it is of me to get attached to someone like T, but I can't help it. I'm too far gone.

He said he'd be out late tonight. He's doing his best to find a way for us to be together—without getting anyone killed in the process. I honestly don't know how he does it all.

He spends his time at different offices throughout the week, something I've noticed because he has me picked up to have lunch with him each day. He seems to be well respected by his employees, though it could actually be more fear on their part. I'm not entirely sure.

And I have no idea what he gets up to most nights. Some evenings he comes home and tells me little bits and pieces, while others he just sneaks in quietly. But when we are together, he finds new positions and ways of making me come apart.

I'm lying in bed, considering whether or not to call Reilly, when I hear the key in the door. I jump up and walk into the hallway, right as the front door is being closed. Then he turns around.

"Oh my God, what the hell happened?" He isn't alone. He's with Neo, who currently has one arm propping Theo upright.

"Ah, we ran into a bit of trouble," Neo says as he leads a bloody and bruised Theo over to my sofa. My new damn sofa.

"A bit?" I shove my way past Neo and fall to my knees. "T, what do I do? Tell me what to do."

"Dolcezza, I'm fine. Never been better. You don't need to do anything."

"Cut the bullshit. You're not fine. Did you call the doctor?" I direct my question to the guy who *doesn't* look like he's gone eight rounds in a ring with Tyson.

"Yeah, he's on the way. Trust me, Holly, it's not as bad as it looks. He's had worse."

"Really, that's meant to be comforting? Why does he look like this while you barely have a scratch on you?"

"Because I can clearly dodge them better than your boy here. Also, he's a fucking idiot and tried to single-handily take on five Russians by himself. Those fuckers are ruthless. If L hadn't called me, I wouldn't have even known where he was."

"What do you have against the Russians? And how long is it going to take for the doctor to get here?"

"They're fucking scum. That's what. And they're trying to steal our territory. It's nothing for you to worry about, Holly. I've got it handled," Theo says.

"Yeah, I can see that," I counter. "Don't move." I go into the bathroom, grab a damp towel and some aspirin, and fill a glass of water. When I walk back out, I find Theo and Neo whispering heatedly about something. But they both freeze as soon as they notice I'm there. "Don't stop on my account. Here, take these." I hand the aspirin to Theo and start to wipe the towel gently down his blood-caked cheek and over the curve of his jawline.

The whole right side of his face looks like it's been used as a punching bag, his eye is almost swollen shut, and his lip is cut open. "Who did this to you?" I whisper. *I want to return the favor*—the rage that's building up in me is foreign. I've been mad before, but this is different. I want revenge. I want to destroy something. *Someone.*

"I'm fine, dolcezza. I don't like you worrying," Theo says, groaning as he moves to sit up higher on the sofa.

How does he expect me not to worry? Is this going to be a regular occurrence? Theo coming home black and blue, or worse? Can I really sign up to be the supportive girlfriend of someone who leads such a tumultuous life? "I... I'll be back in a sec." I can feel the tears coming on, and I refuse to cry in front of these two men.

Neo has told me (more than once) that I'm queen material. I have no idea what his image of a queen is, but I'm pretty sure I'm not fit to rule anyone. If only he knew how much of an internal struggle I have every day...

Closing myself in my bedroom, I collect my phone from the table. I need to talk to Reilly, but how can I confide in her without giving away who Theo really is? I know she'd be on the next flight over to drag me home if she knew what I'd managed to get myself mixed up in.

I don't want to leave. I don't want to go anywhere

Theo isn't. I also don't want to see him battered and beaten. What do I do? I need a sign.

Now would be a really good time for your guidance, Dylan. I know you help Reilly all the time, so how about you help me just this once?

I swipe at my cheeks. I hate that I cry so easily. It's something I've dealt with my whole life; it's why I avoid any and all situations where confrontation might happen. And now I'm sitting here on my bedroom floor, crying and talking to my dead brother. Yep, Holly 2.0 is working out just fine.

The bedroom door opens, and I don't need to look up to know it's him. I feel him in every fiber of my being. "Dolcezza, I'm sorry. I shouldn't have come here. I should have gone home and got cleaned up first." Theo sits down in front of me and pulls my hands away from my face. "I don't want to upset you. Sei troppo bella per piangere," he whispers as he wipes his thumbs across my cheeks.

"I just needed a second. I'll be fine in a second." I hiccup before looking up at him. And seeing how hurt he is—yeah, that's not helping at all.

"You don't need to be anything other than who you are. What's got you upset?"

"You really don't know? Let me ask you, T: how would you feel if I came home to you in the middle of the night all beaten and battered?"

I watch as his face hardens, as his eyes darken. "I'd be out on the streets burning this fucking city to the ground until I found the fucker who hurt you. And when I did, I'd enjoy every moment of his pain."

"That's exactly how I feel when I see you like this, Theo. I have this overwhelming urge to hunt someone down, these violent thoughts running through my mind." I shake my head. This is not me. I'm the wall-flower. I'm not violent. I'm not vengeful. "I don't know how to handle these kinds of feelings. They're over-whelming. I've never wanted to hurt anyone in my life. But right now, I really, really want to hurt someone." Theo smiles at me. *He's bloody insane.* "Why are you smiling?" I ask, frustrated.

"You, *mia regina senza nome*, are growing your wings. You are becoming who you were born to be."

"And who's that?"

"The queen of one of the world's most notorious mafia families. *My* queen."

"I'm not a queen, Theo. I shut myself in my room, because I can't even stand to look at you when you're hurt like this. How is that queen material?"

"It's because you care, bella. That's why it hurts you the way it does. You can feel however you feel, Holly. There is nothing wrong with it. But know that, no matter what, I'll do whatever I can to prevent you from ever getting your hands dirty. You might want to hurt someone right now, but I'd have you tied to the fucking bed before I'd ever let you go out on a rampage."

I look over at the bed, the idea of being tied down

to it not an unpleasant one at all. "Are you really going to be okay?" I ask him.

"It'll take a lot more than this to knock me out of the game. I'll be fine."

Theo is passed out in bed. The doctor came and looked him over. Apparently, they're all a bunch of superficial injuries. I tried to tell Theo he needed a second opinion—to which, the doctor glared at me and told me I didn't know what I was talking about. Then the grumpy old man snapped his medical bag shut and left. Neo followed behind him, though I half expected him to come back to check on his cousin. But he didn't.

I helped Theo shower and made him climb into bed. But I haven't been able to get to sleep myself. The sun is starting to shine through the windows, and I'm exhausted. I have a meeting at my new school today. And I have to be there in... three hours. My eyes are probably puffy from crying and the lack of sleep. *Great, that's exactly the kind of first impression I wanted to make on my employers.* I'm due to start next week, which I'm thankful for, because I could honestly use the distraction. The only thoughts that seem to reside in my mind lately are that of Theo.

"Mmm, your thinking woke me up, Hol." Theo's

gravelly voice has me turning my head towards him. The arm he's had thrown over me all night tightens as he drags my body closer to his.

"Sorry, I'm just nervous."

"What about?"

"I have a meeting at the school today. I look like crap. And I just... I don't know. What if they don't like me?"

"Dolcezza, if they don't like you, then they're fucking idiots and I can put a hit out."

I screw my face up at him. I'm sure he's joking. *He has to be, right?* "You are joking, right?" I repeat the question out loud this time. "You wouldn't actually put a hit out on someone, just because they didn't like me."

"Ah, sure, let's go with that." He laughs.

Yeah, not convincing. There's also the tiny detail that he's having *that* dinner. *The engagement announcement.* I feel nauseous every time I think about it. "You have that family dinner tonight, with Lana, right?" I ask, like it's not a fact I've obsessed over.

"Yep, but I'll be here right after. Don't worry about it. It's just a family thing, nothing else."

"It's your wedding date announcement, Theo. That's not just dinner."

"It's not happening. I'm close to figuring a way out of it." I'm not sure he actually is, but for the sake of my heart, I really hope so.

I've met Lana for coffee twice this week. She swears up and down there is no chance in hell she'll ever go through with this marriage, and that if Theo doesn't find a way out of it, then she has something up her sleeve. I want to believe them. They know the world they live in. And I'm just a bystander really. What do I know about the inner workings of the bloody mafia? Nothing, that's what.

"How about we get up, and I take you to Helena's for breakfast before you go to your meeting? *Or...* we could stay here, and I could have you for breakfast."

"Mmm, I think I'll take option two," I murmur as T's head is already traveling south.

Chapter Seventeen

My whole body fucking aches as my mouth trails all the way down Holly's torso. I don't care how much agony I'm in; there is nothing that will stop me from getting my taste of her. I lift her shirt to find her pussy bare, ready, and waiting for me to get my fill. The problem is: it's never enough. No matter how long I spend down here, I want more. I want everything she has to give.

My tongue swipes up the center of her clit, slowly circling around before I thrust it inside her opening. Her sweet juices fill my mouth as I suck, lick, and nibble her. Her moans are music to my ears, giving me all the encouragement I need to continue pushing her over. I bring her to the edge, only to back off slightly until her thighs clamp around my head and her fingers tangle in my hair. She holds my head in place.

"Please," she says.

"Please what?" Lifting my neck slightly, I allow my eyes to meet hers.

"You know what, T. Don't do this to me."

"I have no idea what you're talking about, Holly. All I'm doing is enjoying my breakfast."

"Argh, well, your breakfast isn't a bloody all-day buffet, so hurry up and make me come already."

"Fuck, Holly, I love it when you're feisty. But you should know I'm in charge here—*always*. However, since you asked so nicely, I'll concede."

I dive back in; my teeth graze her clit as I pump two fingers into her. Her walls clamp down around my fingers, sucking them into her pussy and keeping them hostage. I continue to lick as she rides out her first orgasm of the morning. I say *first* because I sure as shit plan on making her come at least another two times before we get out of this bed.

Once she's come down and her body goes limp, I climb back over and line up my cock with her opening. "I fucking love your pussy, Holly. I love eating it, I love fingering it, and I fucking love fucking it," I tell her right before slamming in. I groan, both in pleasure and pain. *Fuck, my body is in worse shape than I thought.* Every thrust fucking hurts, but the pleasure of being inside her is too much to stop. I roll over and pull her on top. "I need you to take charge, dolcezza," I groan.

"Are you okay? We should stop. Shit, T, I'm sorry. I didn't think about your injuries. I'm so sorry. Should I get you something for the pain?"

"What you should do is bounce your pussy up and down on my cock, Holly. I'm fine, never felt better." I place my hands on her hips and start moving her body along my shaft. Her pussy convulses, tightening and sucking me in as deep as it can. "God, you feel so good."

"Just so you know: having you inside me, I've never felt more alive, more connected or more everything. Being with you is just everything, Theo." Her head rolls backwards as her walls clamp tight, and her body goes rigid as she comes.

"Fuck, fuck!" My release follows right along with hers, my cock emptying itself into her tight pussy. Five minutes later, once I've caught my breath, I realize why that time was different. Why she felt better than ever... "Fuck, Holly, I'm sorry. I wasn't thinking."

"What are you talking about?" She turns towards me.

"I didn't use a condom," I confess.

"*We* didn't use a condom, T. You weren't doing

that alone. Don't worry about it. I'm clean. And I'm also on the pill."

"I wasn't worried about you not being clean, Holly. And, really, if I think about it, the idea of knocking you up... of having you barefoot and pregnant in my kitchen is quite appealing."

"I'm glad you think so. Because when I have kids, I want heaps of them."

"When *we* have kids. You won't be having them with anyone who isn't me."

"Mmm, we'll see. You do have an engagement dinner tonight with another woman *who isn't me*."

"Argh, don't remind me."

The last thing I want to be doing right now is playing happy-fucking-families with my dutiful fake fiancée. Lana's been acting strange all night. I know she wants this marriage to happen about as much as I do, which is not at fucking all.

She's nervous about something else though. She's usually good at hiding her thoughts and feelings—not someone to play poker with, that's for sure. But tonight, I can see her hands shake as she picks up her wine glass. It's subtle; most wouldn't notice.

"I'm so excited. This wedding can't come soon

enough. I've been waiting too long for those grandbabies to get here." My mother sighs.

And my immediate thoughts go to Holly, and the fact that I fucked up this morning by not using protection. It's not something I've ever done. *Did* I fuck up though? The idea of her pregnant is appealing in more ways than one. But her being pregnant with me, out of wedlock, is not a good look for my family. It'd also put a huge fucking target on her back. That's the last thing I want for Holly. I'll do anything to protect her.

"Honey, you really outdid yourself tonight. This is delicious," Lana's mother says from across the table.

Lana looks pale; she's got little sweat beads on her eyebrows. "Thank you, Mom. I wanted it to be special." She reaches out and grabs hold of my hand.

I'm taken aback, because we've never shared such an intimate gesture. Her palm's cold, and her hand is still shaking. "What's wrong? Are you sick?" I whisper in her ear.

She gives a slight shake of her head, tears welling up in the corners of her eyes. "I'm sorry," she says.

I don't have time to figure out why she's apologizing before the chaos ensues. My mother screams, Lana's mother squeals, and the combined noise rings through my ears. I look across to my mother, who is holding my father's head in her hands.

She's inconsolable. "Theo, help! He's choking." I jump up and go to my father. He's now foaming at the mouth.

"Someone, help!" Lana's mother yells as she tries to attend to her own husband, who's in equal distress. *What the fuck?*

I look across to Neo; he nods. "Shut the fucking house down. No one leaves," I order above the commotion. My father's body slumps as I watch the life literally drain out of him. I lift my mother into my arms and escort her from the room. On my way, it clicks: *Lana. She did this.* "Fuck!" She hasn't moved from her spot at the table; she's staring at her father's lifeless body. "Mom, I'm sorry. I will find out who did this. I will fucking destroy whoever did this," I promise, knowing full well I could do no such thing. I may not be in love with the girl, but she's one of my best friends. I could never hurt her.

But how the fuck do I protect her from this? She fucked up. She just single-handedly killed two out of the five heads of the New York mafia.

As I guide my mother to one of the couches in the living room, I realize what this means for me.

My father is dead.

I'm his heir.

I'm now the boss.

Fuck, I was not ready for this. Did I want to find a way out of marrying Lana? Fuck yes. However, I did not want my father to fucking die as a result.

It's irrational, but I want to fucking destroy something. I know I can't harm the person responsible. But I will never forgive her for this either. Lana might as well be dead. Because to me, she fucking is.

"Somebody needs to fucking pay. Who the fuck thinks they can do this to us?" I get up and pace the room.

"T, I'm sorry. What do you need me to do?" Neo asks, standing in the doorway.

"Line up the fucking kitchen staff. *Now!*" I yell as I pick up a lamp and throw it across the room.

"On it, boss." He pivots immediately and heads towards the back of the house.

Boss... He's always joked about it. But this time it rings true. Fuck! I'm not ready for this shit. I was supposed to have years left, years of being the underboss, years of not being in charge of the whole fucking family.

"Mom, stay here. Don't come into the kitchen." I go to walk out.

"Theo, make them pay," my mother says from behind me.

"I will." By the time I get to the kitchen, Neo has all ten of the kitchen staff lined up against the pristine white cabinets. "Who the fuck served that food to my father?" I yell as I pull my gun from my waistband.

They each shake their heads. They know their time is limited. Not a single one of them will make it out of this kitchen alive. But I'll let them think they have a chance.

"Someone better start fucking talking!" I aim

slightly above their heads, emptying the magazine into the cabinets. Shards of broken glass rain down on them like open skies. Their screams seep into my veins. I fucking love their fear. I need this. I need to cause someone pain. And right now, it's them. Reloading, I walk up to the first woman. "What's your name, sweetheart?"

She cries out, "P-please don't hurt me. I-I didn't do anything."

I fire at her knee, watching as she falls to the floor. Bending down, I grab hold of her ponytail and pick her face up to meet mine. "Wrong answer. I asked what your fucking name was!"

"T-T-Tina."

"Tina, see? That wasn't so fucking hard, was it, darling?" She shakes her head no. Tears are streaming down her cheeks. I have a slight moment of guilt? Or is it remorse? This woman probably had no idea what she was being used for. But that tiny flicker is gone in a heartbeat as I remember my old man foaming at the mouth. "You see, one of you served the food that killed my father. And not just *my father,* but the Don of the Valentino family. Do you have any idea what you've done?"

Again, she gestures no.

"You wouldn't." I stand up, aim the end of the barrel directly at her head, and pull the trigger. I watch as the blood pools around her body before turning to face the nine remaining staff members. "Now, who's next?" I ask, smiling at them. "No one? No volunteers? Huh, Neo, I thought at least one of them would want an easy way out."

"Ah, T. Can I have a word?" Neo asks.

I look at him, but I'm enjoying this way too much to stop now. Opening the drawers, I search for an instrument before finding a small paring knife. I smile. "Not right now. I'm busy. I don't care if I have to stay here all fucking night—if I have to watch you each go down one by fucking one—either way, you will all fucking pay."

"Um, T, stop. This wasn't their fault." Lana, the last fucking person I need to see right now, enters the kitchen.

I turn and push her up against the cupboard. I press the small blade into the side of her neck. One little push, and I'll have her carotid artery severed. She'll bleed out in seconds. "Tell me, L, how'd you do it?" I whisper.

"I-I got something from my friend—Elena," she stammers out. I know exactly who *her friend* is: Elena Tarkhanov. Up until a few years ago, she was Elena Falcone. I always suspected she killed her own father and husband. She's now married to fucking Konstantin, the head of the Bratva. The fucking Russians.

"What the fuck were you thinking, L?" I step back and pace the kitchen.

"I was thinking I didn't want to end up married to your ass, Theo. It was either them, or me. And I chose me."

"I was fucking working on it. You should have left it alone." By now, everyone in the kitchen knows the truth. It doesn't matter though; not a single one of them will live long enough to tell a soul. "Neo, get her the fuck out of here. I'll fix this for you, L. But you and I— we are done. And so is our friendship."

"I didn't have a choice, T."

"There's always a choice, and you chose wrong."

Half an hour later, I'm tearing up Lana's place. The kitchen looks like a fucking slaughterhouse. *I guess, technically, it is.* I'm covered in blood. And I've got so much rage left in me. I know I'm losing my goddamn mind. I can feel myself skidding into dangerously uncontrolled territory. I'm always able to rein those emotions in, but right now, my hold's slipping.

Neo had the newly appointed widows taken back to my father's house. I don't know where Lana's disappeared to. But if she's smart, she'll run and not show her face around me again.

I'm lifting another vase, to throw it across the room, when I hear *her* voice. "Theo?"

Chapter Eighteen

Holly

Have you ever had that feeling in your gut that something horrible was happening, but you had no idea what it was or how to stop it?

I have that right now. I don't know what exactly, but I can sense that something terrible has happened. At first, I called Reilly. I thought something was wrong with her. But she was fine. Usually, when I feel this, it's because Reilly is upset or in trouble.

She could tell I wasn't okay. I had to make up some bullshit, saying I was nervous about starting the new job. I don't think she bought into it, but she did let it go. I'm not okay though. I have no idea what to do other than walk up and down the tiny space of my living room, clenching my phone in my hands.

I've tried calling Theo. I've actually called him ten times, and he hasn't answered. Maybe I could walk down to the coffee shop and ask Helena if she knows anything? Or if she has another way of getting ahold of him?

I'm more than likely overreacting. This feeling could just be my ugly jealousy rising up because of where and what Theo is doing right now. I know he and Lana both swear black and blue that they will not go through with this wedding... But there is this small voice in the back of my head telling me they will... if they can't find a way out.

Neither of them will have a choice.

I've learnt a few things about the way Theo's family works over the last week, including the fact that they have very strict traditions and rituals. Do I understand them? Absolutely not. But I've fallen head over heels in love with this man. It's an irrational, soul-consuming love—unlike anything I've ever experienced. And if I were to lose Theo, I know I'd never find anything like it again. This man is my once-in-a-lifetime love. The one all the fairy tales sell you on. Except, instead of a charming prince with a fancy castle, I scored myself a dark prince with a throne built on secrets, lies, blood, and crime. Though, from what Theo tells me, there's much more than that to his empire. There's also loyalty, trust, and faith.

I try to call him again and again, but his phone goes straight to voicemail. I don't know if I'd survive if something were to happen to him. I'm not strong like Reilly. I can't imagine what she went through when Bray was shot—the months she spent at his bedside while he was in a coma and wouldn't wake up. I thought I understood her pain back then. But it's only now, as I am plagued by this fear of something happening to Theo, that I truly get it. And the fact that he came home last night beaten and bloodied is not helping. What if he's been hurt again?

I know something is wrong. He needs me, and I don't know how to get to him or where to even start looking. I'm resigned to heading over to Helena's when there's banging on the door. *Thank God. He's here!* Swinging it open, I call out, "Theo, where the hell..." My words trail off and my stomach drops. It's not him. Instead, Neo is standing there. *Alone.* I shake my head. "No... Where is he, Neo? What happened?"

"Holly, he's okay... In sorts. I need you to come with me though. *Something* has happened. And I believe you're the only person who can actually help him right now."

I don't think twice about it. I pick up my keys from the hall table and lock the door. "What's going on? Where is he?"

"I'll tell you in the car, not here." Neo guides me out of the building. I struggle to keep up with his pace.

Once we're in the car, he has it screeching out into traffic. Horns beep and people curse before they quickly turn their heads the other way, like they didn't see anything. That's something that happens a lot when I'm with Theo: people don't make eye contact with him. I've even seen some purposely cross the street to avoid his path.

"Okay, tell me what the hell happened? What's wrong?" I'm going out of my mind, conjuring up all the ways Theo could be hurt.

"His father was murdered at dinner, along with Lana's," Neo answers.

"What? How? Is Theo... is he hurt?"

"He's fine. They were poisoned. Theo's not taking it too well, which is understandable."

"Well, his father just died—of course he's not fucking taking it well. What did you expect?" I will go down defending Theo no matter what. Even if it's to his cousin.

"You don't understand, Holly. When Theo doesn't handle things *well*, it gets very messy very quickly."

"You're right: I don't understand. So, simplify it for me, in layman's terms."

"He's gone on a rampage. Lana's house is a fucking

bloodbath. Prepare yourself, because the Theo you know is not the same man you're about to walk in on. Right now, he's hurting and if you love him like you claim, then you need to help him."

"He doesn't know you came to get me, does he?" I ask.

"He's not gonna want you to see him like this. But I didn't know what else to do. This is the worst I've ever seen him."

"Okay, tell me what to do? How do I help him?"

"You accept him without judgment. He was prepared to go to war to keep you, Holly. You have to be prepared to do the same. Whatever you see, whatever you hear when we get there, you need to block that shit out and focus only on Theo."

"Okay," I whisper. My mind is still stuck on the word *bloodbath*. I'm not sure I'm strong enough for this. Maybe Theo's father was right, in pairing him with someone from his world. I don't know if I'm cut out for it. I'm second guessing myself the whole way, before I realize Neo is finally pulling into a gated estate. "Where are we?" I ask.

"This is Lana's house, or what's left of it... Stay behind me. I don't know what state he's in."

I nod my head as I follow him, up the stairs and through the entrance of the house. That is, until I hear the scream. Shoving my way past Neo, I run down the hall, only stopping when I get to an open doorway. I see the destruction before I see *him*.

"Theo?" I call out, just as he's about to throw a vase. Turning around, he stares at me. Yes, he's covered in blood and his shirt is torn open. But that's not what gets me; it's the broken look in his eyes. The torment I can see deep within him. I run and throw my arms around his shoulders. Theo drops the vase at our feet, and I jump up and cling to him. I may not know what to do, but I know I want to hold him. I want to be the one he leans on to keep him together. I bury my head in the side of his neck. "I'm so sorry," I whisper.

His arms clutch me tighter as he collapses to the ground. "How...? What...? You shouldn't be here, Holly."

"There is nowhere else I should be but by your side, T."

"No, this isn't... You shouldn't see this."

I look around before looking back at him. "The only thing I see is you. I see you, Theo. I see that the man I love is hurting. That's what I'm seeing."

"He's dead..." I notice the tears in the corners of his eyes. "I was supposed to have more time. He wasn't supposed to go this early."

"I know." I don't know what else to say. What else to do. I don't know how to help him. If I could take away his pain, I would. *In a heartbeat.*

"No, you don't understand. He's dead. I have to take over now."

"You will do whatever it is you have to do, T. You

will step up and take over, and you'll be the best damn boss this family of yours has ever seen."

"I can't do this. I... what do I do now?"

"Now, you clean yourself up and help your family grieve. You let *yourself* grieve and you take charge."

Theo smiles a sad smile at me. "You really are my unassuming queen."

"I'm not a queen. I'm just me. Tell me how I can help. What can I do?"

"You're doing it," he says, as he holds me tighter while silently sobbing into my neck. I doubt this man has been brought to tears often, and it's breaking my heart.

I can't help but think about how I'd feel if it were *my* father; the guilt I have over not visiting him more often is consuming me. After he went to jail, I couldn't forgive him for leaving us. I hated that he did what he did. I hated that he left Mum, Reilly, and me alone. But right now, I could really use his guidance.

"I love you. That will never change, no matter what happens," I tell Theo. We're lying in his bed. After about an hour of holding on to each other on the floor, Theo stood up and carried me out of the house. He put me in his car and drove back to his apartment in silence.

"I don't know what's going to happen next, but you are mine. I'm not letting you go." His fingertips play with the ends of my hair. He does this a lot. "Will you come with me to my parents' house in the morning? I need to check on my mother."

"Do you think it's wise for me to go there?" I ask.

"I don't give a shit if it's wise. I need to be there, and I'm not ready to *not* be next to you."

"Okay, if you want me to come with you, I will." I lean forward and gently meet his lips. "Promise me something."

"What?"

"If it gets dangerous, if it's a choice between you and me, you'll choose yourself. I don't want you to go to war or put yourself in danger for me."

"I can't promise you that, Holly. I will always choose us. You are a part of me that I can't let go of. So, if it comes down to it, it's going to be you. It's always going to be you."

"I'm scared I'm losing you already. And I don't know how to stop it. But even if I do, if something were to happen, I wouldn't change a thing."

"You're not losing me. I'm yours. *That much,* I can promise."

Chapter Nineteen

I'm gripping Holly's hand tighter than I should. I can't help it. I'm leaning on her strength right now. She thinks she's weak, but she is stronger than any man I know.

Climbing the steps of my family home, with Holly by my side, I almost expect my father to walk out and demand to know who she is and why I've brought her here. He's not going to walk out though; he's never going to walk out again.

The front doors swing open and Teresa wraps her arms around me. She's sobbing. "I'm so sorry, Mr. Valentino." She quickly pulls away and straightens out her dress.

Tugging Holly closer to my side, I ignore my housekeeper's sympathies and introduce my soon-to-be queen. "Teresa, this is Holly. Make sure she gets anything she needs. Holly, this is my family's house-keeper—Teresa."

Holly looks from me to the distraught woman in front of us. Then she pulls her hand free of mine and hugs Teresa. "I'm sorry for your loss, Teresa. Let me know if there's anything I can do for you." Holly drops the embrace and I'm quick to take her hand again.

"Thank you. Mr. Valentino, your mother is in the library." Teresa steps back to let us through the doors.

"Thank you, Teresa." I offer a nod of my head.

Holly stops in the foyer, wide-eyed. I try to look at the place from her point of view, as someone with new eyes. Clearly no expense has been spared; my mother has a niche for decorating *and* spending my father's money. The floors are white and black marble, while everything else is shades of gold and cream, right down to the huge bouquet of white and cream flowers on every table throughout the foyer.

"It's so beautiful, Theo. I can't believe this is where

you grew up." She turns, eyeing the elaborate winding staircase.

"I'll give you a tour soon. Come on." I pull her through the foyer towards the library.

I find my mother sitting on her favorite chair, with a glass of wine in her hand. She's staring off into space.

"Mamma." I walk up to her and take the glass, placing it on the table next to her before kissing her on each cheek.

"Theo. You're okay?" she asks as she inspects my face. It's still discolored from my run-in the other night.

"I'm doin' fine. Mamma, I want you to meet my friend—Holly." I stand and pull our quiet onlooker forward.

"It's a pleasure to meet you, Mrs. Valentino. I'm sorry for your loss."

"I'm sure you are, my dear." My mother rises to her feet, and her hand comes out and slaps me across the face before I can even think to stop it. I knew she wouldn't be impressed with Holly, but this reaction is a bit dramatic, even for my mother.

"Mamma, what the fuck?" I instinctually step in front of Holly. I will protect her at all costs, no matter the aggressor.

"Please tell me you didn't do this, Theo. It can't be. What have you done?" my mother cries out.

Wrapping my arms around her, I hold her still. "It wasn't me, Mamma, I swear to you. It wasn't me."

"Who was it then?"

"I can't tell you that." *I really can't.*

"The family will want answers, Theo. What are you going to tell them?"

"The truth: that the person responsible has been dealt with." What the fuck *am* I going to tell them? And Lana's family? I'm sure Lana's brother, John, is flying in from Italy as we speak. He's been overseeing the international family businesses for the past few years. I can't let him know it was Lana; there is no doubt in my mind he'd execute her himself. "What arrangements need to be made?" I shift the conversation.

"Father Thomas is visiting for lunch. You'll stay and help me organize the service and viewing. *Your friend* needs to go home, Theo. She doesn't belong here." My mother picks up her drink and walks out of the room.

"I, um, do you want me to go? I don't want to cause trouble, T."

"You're not leaving, Holly. I don't care what anyone says. Your place is right beside me; you belong with me."

"Mmm, I know that. You know that. But your mother clearly has other ideas, and she's grieving right now. I don't want to upset her any further. That being said, I'd like to cut the hand off that slapped you." Holly runs her fingertips over my cheek.

"My mother has never done that before. She's not usually like this. You're right: she's grieving. However, she will give you the respect you deserve. I won't allow anyone to disrespect you, Holly. Not even my mother." I wrap my arms around her and pull her into my chest. My head rests above hers, and I breathe in her coconut and vanilla scent.

It's calming; she's calming. Right now, my body is drained, and my mind is running a mile a minute with everything I have to fucking do. I'm not even sworn in as the Don yet, and I'm already exhausted.

"Theo, I need a word." This comes from my Uncle Gabe, who is also my father's consigliere. *Was* my father's consigliere... I guess, now he's mine. If I choose to keep him on in that role...

The position is basically the advisor to the Don; he's trusted and responsible for assisting in settling family disputes and counseling on a range of business matters. I trust my Uncle Gabe. He is Neo's father after all.

With Neo stepping up as my underboss, I believe Gabe would have the family's best interests at heart. *Always.* He'd do anything for his son, no matter what. Something I was always a little jealous of. As I mentioned, my pops was a decent father, but he was a far better mafia boss—the kind of man who'd put a bullet in his own son's head if the kid did anything that wasn't acceptable to the family. That's where the two differed: my uncle wouldn't just kill for his children; he'd die for them.

"Ah, sure. Uncle Gabe, this is Holly. Holly, Uncle

Gabe, also known as Neo's father." I wave my hand back and forth between the two.

"Hi." Holly gives a shy wave. She's withdrawn and on guard after meeting with my mother. I don't blame her; I would be too.

"It's nice to meet you, Holly. I'm sorry, but I do have urgent matters to discuss with Theo."

"Of course. I'll just, ah, wait..." Holly looks around the room as her sentence trails off.

"Hold on." I take out my phone and call Neo.

He answers on the first ring. "Boss?"

"Where are you?" I ask.

"Just pulled up out front of your parents. Where are you?"

"Meet me in the library." I hang up and turn back to Holly.

"Dolcezza, I'm sorry. I do have to go and sort some things out. I'll have Neo wait in here with you. I won't be long." I kiss her forehead just as my cousin enters.

"You summoned me?" he calls out.

Uncle Gabe slaps him across the back of the head. "That's the boss you're speaking to, son. Show some respect."

"Right, sorry, boss. What do you need?" Neo smirks at me.

"Shut up. Stay in here with Holly, and keep my mother away from her."

Walking into my father's office feels wrong. He's not here—though he should be. I purposely sit on the sofa. I'm not sitting behind that desk, a fact that doesn't escape Uncle Gabe.

"Theo, I know you just lost your father. But the family, the men, they just lost their leader. You need to step up and take charge immediately. Show them that this family will not falter under attack."

"I know." I run my hands through my hair. "What do I do, Gabe? I don't know what I'm supposed to do here," I confess.

"Yes, you do. You've been preparing for this your whole life. You *are* a leader, Theo. So, you lead."

"What if I can't do it?"

Gabe watches me silently for a few minutes, contemplating his next words. He's always careful when he speaks; it's what makes him good at his job. "Do you love her?"

Okay, not the question I was expecting... "Who?"

"Don't play dumb with me, son. It doesn't suit you. The redhead you've got holed up in the library."

"Holly? Yeah, I do." I look towards the door. I'm itching to get back out there. *To get to her*.

"The first thing your enemies are going to see is your weakness. She's your weakness."

"You're wrong. She's my strength. Right now, she's the only thing holding me together."

"I don't mean it like that. If your enemy wants to hurt you, they will go after her to do it."

"You think I haven't thought of that already?" I ask, a little pissed off.

"So, what are you going to do about it?"

"I'm not getting rid of her. I don't care what anyone fucking says. She's mine. I'm keeping her."

"First off: she's not a fucking pet dog, Theo. You don't get to keep a woman. She *lets* you be the one to warm her bed at night. Second: I'm not suggesting you get rid of her, quite the opposite actually. Take your vow to the family and then marry her. Show them that you're ready to rule with the same strength your father did. Show them that you're not someone to fuck with, Theo. That's how you protect her."

Marry her? Well, fuck, that's an idea I could actually get on board with. The question is: would Holly?

"What do you know about this arranged marriage deal with Lana? What was Pops getting out of it?"

"Nothing, he was tight-lipped on that. Had a few meetings alone with Big John. I have no idea what the fuck those two were cooking up with *that* plan. But whatever it was, I'm sure we'll find out soon enough."

"And you're suggesting I don't follow along with my father's orders? That I don't marry Lana?" I'm asking to see if he slips up, to see if he *does* know something he's not telling me.

"No, I'm *advising* you to marry someone you love. A marriage is forever, Theo. You do not want to end up in a miserable one."

"Okay. Any ideas on how you get a woman you've only known for a week to agree to marry you?" I ask, rising up to my full height.

"Not a fucking clue, but from what I saw, that girl is smitten. I'm sure you'll figure something out."

"Thanks."

"Theo, it will all be okay. You'll do great. I've been looking forward to this day for a very long time. I'm sorry your pops ain't here to witness it, but I know you'll do him proud." Gabe hugs me before kissing both of my cheeks.

"Thank you."

Chapter Twenty

Holly

"I'm really okay to wait here, T. You should go have lunch with your mother and help her. I'll be fine." I leave out the part that I'd much rather stay here in this library with all these books, than have to endure another run in with his mother. I get she's grieving—she's just lost her husband—but I haven't done anything to warrant her instant hatred. I've never met a boyfriend's parents before. This is all very uncharted territory for me, and to be meeting them under such conditions is not ideal, to say the least.

"Nonsense, you're coming with me."

"Your mother doesn't want me there, Theo. It's okay. I don't mind waiting," I try again.

"Holly, dolcezza." Theo runs his fingertips over my hair, tucking the loose strands behind my ear. "I need you there. Please."

Well, bloody hell, when he puts it like that, how can I possibly say no? "Okay, but if at any point you need me to disappear into another room and give you and your mother privacy, just tell me."

"I don't ever need or want privacy from you, dolcezza. If I could get away with it, I'd have you hand-cuffed to me so we'd never have to be apart." Theo smiles, but it doesn't reach his eyes.

"Sure, give it a go and see how far you get with that."

"Like I said, if I could get away with it. Come on, let's do this so we can go home."

We've been waiting for Theo's mother to come and join us for lunch for around twenty minutes. Theo's grip on my hand under the table is tight. Every now and then, he'll loosen it slightly for a moment before tightening his hold again. I'm not sure if he's afraid I'll disappear (or leave) and this is his way of ensuring I can't. Or if he just needs the support. Either way, I'm not going anywhere. If he wants me here, then I'll be here.

"I'm sorry, Father. She shouldn't be too much longer," Theo says to the priest sitting across from us. It's a little unsettling for me. I'm not sure why. I'm not an overly religious person, so to have a priest among us is strange. I feel like I should be confessing all my sins or something. As I think of everything I've ever done wrong in my life, I glance at Theo and wonder what his list must look like. Yet, he sits here as cool as a cucumber—as if butter wouldn't melt in his mouth.

"It's okay, Theo. We all grieve in our own way. How are you holding up?"

"I'm fine."

"It's okay to not be fine, son. You've just lost your father. You've had a lot of responsibility that's just fallen directly onto your shoulders. If there was ever a time to not be fine, this would be it."

"I'm fine," Theo repeats.

"Very well then. Holly, how long have you been in New York?" Father Thomas asks me.

"Ah, a little over a week," I answer quietly. Why do I feel so judged by everyone in this house?

"And how long have you known Theo here?"

"A little over a week," I answer.

Father Thomas looks between Theo and me for a moment. "Well, perhaps when the time comes, you'll allow me the pleasure of marrying you," he offers.

I choke on the water I was sipping, spitting it out all over the table. I can feel my face heating up.

"Holly, breathe. You're okay." Theo rubs my back. "I'm glad the thought of marrying me incites such a reaction," he says sarcastically. His eyes look hurt though. Does he think I wouldn't want to marry him?

"I was caught off guard—that's all. If you were to actually ask, the answer would probably be yes."

"Probably, huh? I like my chances. I'll keep that in mind." Theo kisses my forehead, then leans in and whispers, "I'm not letting you go. Married or not, Holly, you're mine. Forever."

"Good, because I have a no returns or refunds poli-cy." This actually gets a smile out of him, a genuine smile.

"Theo, I thought I told you to take out the trash." His mother sits at the table in an elegant black gown.

Theo slams his hand down and stands up. "Cut the shit, Ma. I won't allow you to disrespect Holly. You can either get on board, accept her, and show her the respect she fucking deserves. Or we can cut ties now."

I gasp at Theo's sharp words. He's not seriously threatening to cut ties with his own mother, just because she doesn't like me? Surely not. I reach up and grab his arm, pulling him back down into his seat. "Theo, it's okay."

"No, it's not okay, Holly. No one will disrespect you in this family."

"Seriously, Theo, you're acting like a petulant child. It's beneath you, just like your choice of company. Don't worry, your fiancée should be here soon. I've sent a car to collect her."

"You did what?" Theo yells.

"I sent a car for Lana. *Your fiancée.*" His mother smirks at me, as if I'm unaware of his prior arrangement.

"Lana is not welcome in this house. She's also not now—and never has been—my fucking fiancée. That whole bullshit Pops tried to pull, it's over with. The only woman I'll ever marry is sitting right next to me, so start showing your next queen the fucking respect she deserves."

"Queen, *please.* She's not even Italian, Theo. She won't be accepted by anyone."

Okay, I've been working really hard to fight the tears that are pooling in my eyes. I don't like to cry in front of people. I try to save that for when I'm alone. I'm looking around the room for an escape when Theo's hand grips mine. Like an anchor, he's holding me still.

"I'm really sorry for your loss, Mrs. Valentino. I understand I may not be your first choice for your son. But I do love him, more than I ever thought I could love anyone." I don't know why I'm looking for this horrible woman's acceptance. But, for some reason, I am.

"Love? You don't even know him, sweetheart. You're not from this world. You have no idea what you're getting yourself into here. So let me tell you. A life trapped in a gilded cage, that's what *this* is. It might look fancy; it might look like you have everything you need. It's not. And you won't. It's a life sentence; it's always having to look over your shoulder. Always having to be on guard. It's never leaving the house without armed security. Then, when you have children, you have to watch them grow up as they're groomed into this lifestyle. Is that what you want for yourself?"

Well shit... *no* would be my first answer. Then I think about what the alternative is. A white picket fence and a normal guy with a normal job. The life my mum and dad had, before he went to jail. Yet, it still ended in tragedy. That so-called *safe life* doesn't exist. Within a heartbeat, your son or daughter... or brother... could be killed by an irresponsible drunk driver.

Nobody can predict what's going to happen.

"I know what I don't want. What I don't want is a future that doesn't include Theo. If I have to learn the ways of your family, if I have to prove myself over and over again to gain your trust or friendship, then I'll do it. Nothing you say will hurt me more than not being with your son. So, I'll sit here and endure whatever it is you need to throw at me. The alternative, the thought of walking out those doors without him, well, that's not an option for me. *At all.*"

Everyone at the table is silently watching me. Theo brings our joined hands up to his mouth and kisses my wrist.

"Did he tell you what happened to his father? What my son did as his father lay cold on the floor?"

"No..."

"Ma, stop!" Theo shouts across the table.

"No, she should know what she's signing up for. I had to watch my husband choke to death, his own saliva bubbling out of his mouth. Someone poisoned him at dinner. At a *family dinner*. Afterwards, Theo went on a rampage—ten of the kitchen staff were slaughtered in that house last night."

I already knew Theo was a little unhinged when I found him covered in blood. But I didn't care. *I don't care.* When I look at him, I see the man who brings me coffee each morning, the man who has cancelled meetings to make sure he can eat lunch with me every day. I look at the man I know would do anything for me. "It doesn't matter what Theo does or doesn't do in his role within your family. What matters is how he is with me. I can't fault him. You've raised a great man, Mrs. Valentino. And I won't let you or anyone else paint him in any other light. Because that's what he deserves."

"Okay then. Father Thomas, should we discuss the funeral arrangements." Theo's mother seems to drop her issue with me and goes into planning mode, as if a switch has been flicked.

For the next hour, I sit there, holding on to Theo's

hand while he and his mother go back and forth about the arrangements and who's doing what. It's a lot. By the sounds of it, this funeral is a bigger deal than any other I've attended. I never got a chance to meet his father, but it seems a lot of other people have. They're expecting at least five hundred attendees to show up to the service. I don't even know that many people...

"Thank you, Father Thomas, for your time." Theo stands and shakes the priest's hand. I watch as the older man holds on to Theo while whispering a prayer. When he's done, they both make the sign of the cross.

I wouldn't have pegged Theo for being a religious person. I'm wondering what else I don't know about him. I guess we have time to find out.

The funeral has been scheduled for Saturday—five days away—to allow the overseas relatives time to fly in. It's the Saturday before I start at the school.

I'm going to have to do some class prep work this week, so I have the weekend free to be with Theo. That's if he wants me in attendance...

Chapter Twenty-One

The early hours of the morning are fast becoming my favorite part of the day. Lying here next to a peacefully sleeping Holly is the best way to start my morning. She's my rock, when I thought I'd be hers. Right now though, I need her like I've never needed anyone else.

It's during these early hours that I get uninterrupted time to admire her beauty. And to thank God for sending her to me. I don't deserve this woman, but I sure as fuck am keeping her. The last couple of days have been hell, while Holly's been the light that brings me back from the darkness.

"Mmm, good morning." Her eyes flicker open, flashing me those green emeralds I love to get lost in.

"Buongiorno, bella." I push her loose tendrils off her back, before leaning in and kissing her lips.

"I love it when you speak Italian to me. What does that mean?"

"Good morning, beautiful."

"I'm sure I look like crap right now. It was a wild night." Her hands come up to smooth down her hair—which is a tangled mass of curls—sprawled out on the pillow beneath her. The red strands are bright and vibrant, a contrast to the white pillow.

"Ogni volta che ti guardo, diventi sempre più bella." I roll over, positioning myself on top of her before repeating my phrase in English, "Every time I look at you, you only get more beautiful."

"Thank you." Her eyes dart to the side. I've noticed that she finds it hard to take compliments. It's why I make an effort to do so as often as possible. It's not a hardship, when every word I speak is the truth.

I kiss along the side of her neck. "Dalla testa ai piedi, la tua bellezza si vede." Pulling the sheet down, I watch as her naked chest comes into view. I cup each breast in my hands and kiss the spot where her heart is. "Ma è la tua bellezza qui dentro che amo di più."

The best thing about translating my words for her? I get to tell her twice. "From your head to your toes, your beauty can be seen." My fingertips trace a heart shape over where hers lies beneath her skin. "But it's your beauty in here that I love the most."

"How is it that you're still single? How have you not been snatched up yet and locked away?" Holly asks.

"Dolcezza, I'm far from single. I'm as taken as taken gets." Does she think *she's* single? Fuck that.

"That's not what I meant. I meant up until I came along, obviously. How did you get by without being kidnapped and held in some woman's basement?"

"Do you want to kidnap me and lock me in your basement, Holly?" I laugh.

"The thought *has* crossed my mind. But then I remember you're a mob boss, and I'd likely have an army of your loyal soldiers out after me."

"I have a feeling you'd outsmart every soldier I have. You don't have to worry though. I'd go into your basement willingly."

"Huh, maybe I should buy a house with a basement somewhere. In the meantime, I may not have a basement, but I do have you and I plan to take full advantage of this work of art you call a body." Her hands travel down the small space between us.

One of her palms wraps around my cock—my already *painfully hard* cock. "Ah, fuck, Hol. Keep doing that," I moan as she continues to stroke up and down.

I'm leaking precum all over her fingers, and I watch in awe as she brings the tips to her mouth. "I never thought I could like the taste of a man as much as I do right now. I don't just like it. *I crave it*. I crave you." She sucks her fingers clean before pushing me onto my back.

"Get comfy. I might be a while," she says as her tongue leaves a wet trail down the center of my abs. She returns her grip to my cock, while her tongue slips out, licking right along the slit of my tip.

"Mmm. God." I take hold of her hair, lifting it away so I can see her face. She never ceases to amaze me. The sight of her mouth agonizingly full, as she wraps her lips around me and guides my cock as far back in her throat as humanly possible, is beyond words. She works me slowly, licking the underside and around the tip with each up and down motion she dispenses. "Fuck, Hol, your mouth is a fucking world treasure."

I feel her giggle, the vibrations running straight through my cock.

"Adoro vedere la tua bocca piena del mio cazzo." I know it turns her on when I speak Italian to her. She has no idea I've just said that *I love seeing her mouth full of my cock*. But her little moans in response tell me she likes what she hears—whether she understands it or not. "Sì, sì, sì. Merda, che si sente bene." Her hand cups my balls, applying just the right amount of pressure. "Shit, I'm going to come, Holly." I offer her a warning in a language she knows, though I'm not sure why I bother anymore. She never backs off. She takes everything I have to give, swallowing every drop as I empty myself into her.

Fucking hell, talk about seeing stars.

I'm catching my breath when she climbs back up my body. "I'm giving you a five-minute break before I expect you to be ready again."

"Yes, ma'am." I salute her. She falls onto the bed next to me, laughing. I roll over so I'm on top of her. "I love your laugh. I want to hear it every day for the rest of my life."

"Well, that seems like an awfully long time, T."

"Meh, it's hit or miss in my line of work." My joke is not well received—*guess I need to read the audience better.*

"That's not funny. You aren't allowed to die, Theo. If you do, I'm going to find a necromancer to bring you back to life, just so I can shoot you myself."

"Don't worry, I have no plans of leaving you. Ever."

"Stage-five clinger. Got it."

"When it comes to you, I'm a fucking stage-ten clinger, dolcezza." I can feel my cock harden again. I run my fingertips around her clit a few times before pushing one inside her. *She's fucking drenched.* "Fuck, you're drenched, dolcezza," I say aloud. "Are you in need of a little release? I'm sure I can help you out with that." I smirk as I add a finger and pump harder while rubbing my thumb around her clit.

"Yes, Theo. Oh, God, don't stop." Her palm wraps around my wrist, holding my hand to her as she rides my fingers. Her hips start moving in time with my thrusts.

"La cosa più bella che abbia mai visto." My teeth graze her ear. "Hottest thing I've ever fucking seen."

"Oh God." Her body seizes up, and her scream bounces through the room. She calls out my name. I'm the one who did this to her. I'm the only fucking one who will do this to her.

Just as she's coming down from her orgasm, I push my cock forward. One quick thrust, and I'm buried deep. "Sposami?" I whisper while I'm still bottomed out inside her.

Holly lifts her legs, wrapping them around my waist. "Huh? What does that mean?"

"Sposami, perfavore?" It's almost like a prayer leaving my lips. I need her to say *yes*. I'll keep asking every day until she does. My forearms are next to her head, bracing my full weight above her. We lock eyes. "I said: *Marry me? Marry me, please?*"

I see her lip quiver. Shit, I've gone and made her fucking cry. I hate seeing her cry, and she does it often. My girl has such a sensitive soul.

"I-I don't know what to say. Hold on." She twists her body and leans over the bed to reach for her phone.

What the hell? I ask her to marry me, and she's

looking for her cell? Who the fuck does she think she's calling?

I watch her type something, then she looks back at me as she reads from the screen: "Sì, mille volte sì." She butchers the fuck out of the pronunciation of every single word. But I got enough to know what she said. What her answer is. *Yes. A thousand times yes.*

I've never felt so elated, so relieved and content. "I love you. Thank you."

"No thanks required. I'm totally the one scoring big time in this deal. You are a hot commodity, Theo. I think I read something about you being *New York's most eligible and desired bachelor* somewhere."

"Don't believe everything you read in the tabloids—they like to make shit up."

"Oh, so you're not the most eligible bachelor? Who is? I should go look for him."

I raise my eyebrows at her. "Only if you want to sign *his* death certificate. And I won't just kill any man who touches you, Holly. I'll fucking destroy them, and I'll enjoy every moment of slow torture. I'll have Doc keep them alive, so I can *keep* working them over. And over again."

"That's... *graphic.* I was joking, Theo. I'd never even look at another man. I'm all in."

"*We're* all in."

She said yes. I'm still on cloud nine as I watch her eat a bagel across the table from me.

"Can you stop! I'm starting to get a complex."

"Stop what?" I smile.

"Staring at me like that."

"Like what?"

"Like you're trying to see into my soul."

"I don't need to see into your soul. I know your soul, Holly, because it's the other half of mine." She won't admit it, but she loves it when I say my—what she calls—*Hallmark lines.* I'm just speaking what's on my mind. Every single thing is the truth.

"So, what's on the agenda today?" she asks.

I shrug. "Boring business shit you wouldn't want to know." Even if she did want to know, I can't fucking tell her a thing. I won't have her implicated in any less-than-legitimate business dealings. If I go down, I go down alone. She'll have plausible deniability every time. I know the Feds are already waiting for me to fuck up. Word's gotten out that Pops died, and I've taken over. Two out of the five families have new bosses this week—that's a big fucking deal.

Everyone's on edge: either waiting for a war, or seeing who's going to crumble under the pressure. I know they're all looking for me to fuck up. I'm young. The youngest Don in the history of the Valentino family.

I don't care what I have to do, how many hours I have to work. I will prove that I deserve this position. That it's not mine just because I was born into it. I fucking earned it with blood, sweat, and my fucking sanity.

"Mmm, well, I have some prep work to do for school next week. I'm so excited. I've never taught third-graders, but I'm looking forward to the change. I mean, how different can they be from the fifth-graders I'm used to teaching, right?"

"You know you don't have to work. I'll take care of you." It doesn't matter to me if she works or not. But the disgust on Holly's face tells me it *definitely* matters to her.

Chapter Twenty-Two

Holly

"I may not be as financially secure as you are, T. But trust me, I'm fine. I do not now—nor will I ever—need you to *take care of me,* as you so eloquently offered," I repeat the sentiment I told him when he paid my bill that first time. "If you're looking for someone to be a stay-at-home wife and tend to your every desire, then look elsewhere. Because that's not me. I love my job. I didn't complete a master's degree to waste it. So, you can take your suggestion and shove it where the sun doesn't shine." I smile, even though my blood is boiling at the thought of him just wanting to chain me down.

"Okay, dolcezza, relax. I was merely being informative. I know you don't need me to take care of you. I've seen your trust fund, Holly. It's just, *typically*, the women in our family don't work. They raise children—that's a full-time job in itself."

"Oh, so now you want me to be your breeding cow?" I fold my arms over my chest. The smirk on Theo's face is pissing me off nearly as much as his misguided expectations.

"Holly, you're taking everything I'm saying the wrong way. If and when we have children, I would expect you to raise them yourself. I can hire nannies, but nothing beats being raised by loving parents. I assumed you would want to stay home with our kids."

"You *assumed*. When you assume, you make an ass out of U and Me," I echo the words my mum used to tell us. "Stop looking at my chest and stop smirking like that."

"Okay. But even I'm only capable of so much. When you cross your arms and push your tits out, it's like a fucking offering I can't turn down. I'm thinking about how I want to slide my cock between your tits and spill my cum all over them."

Well, great, now I'm thinking about that too.

"Damn it, T. Now you've gone and made my panties wet." I laugh at the instant change in his demeanor.

"I can help you out with that. Scoot a little closer." He pats the seat next to him.

"Not a chance in hell. There's a lot I'd let you talk me into. But doing anything like what's going through your mind, here, in this café—yeah, not happening. Besides, I have to get home and get started on work."

"Come with me today. Bring your laptop. You can work from my office."

"I doubt I'd get much done, and besides, I'd just be in your way."

"Holly, you are never in my way. Come with me, please."

"What will your staff think? Bring your girlfriend to work day isn't a thing, T."

"Fiancée. You're not my girlfriend, Holly. You're my fiancée, and the staff won't say a damn thing about it. The best part about being the boss is: I make the fucking rules. Bring your fiancée to work day is now *a thing*. Come on, we'll walk back to your apartment and grab your belongings."

Fiancée... When he says that word, my heart skips a beat all its own. Shit, I haven't even called Reilly yet. Should I tell her about this... development? She's going to try to talk sense into me. I know it. And this isn't something I want to be talked out of doing. I want Theo. I want to be his. I want him to be mine. I don't care what he does for his job, or his family. When he's with me, he's not T, the mafia boss. He's just T, the doting boyfriend—now fiancée—who will do anything to make me happy.

I stand and let him guide me out of the café. I really need to learn how he always ends up getting his way. Here I was, refusing to go and work from his office with him, but now I'm walking back to my apartment to collect my laptop to do just that.

Am I that much of a pushover? I'd like to think not. But he sure does have a way of talking me into anything.

If I really think about it though, I want to go with him. I don't like when we part ways during the day or night so he can go to work. I get he has a big load. And right now, with what's going on in his family, it's even heavier. But he still manages to set aside time for me. If I can make it a little bit easier on him by going and spending the day working from his office, then I'll do it. On the other hand, I'm not so sure I'll get much done when he's around; he's so bloody distracting. I'd be lying if I said seeing him in boss mode, the few times I've been at his office for lunch, isn't a huge turn-on.

"Maria, move the meeting with Carlo to the boardroom." T's voice brings me out of my own thoughts. Surprisingly, I've managed to block him out, mostly, and concentrate on the lesson plans I've been writing up.

"Mr. Valentino, there is currently a meeting in progress with the advertising department in the boardroom."

"Fuck, well, find another room to accommodate us. My office is unavailable for the rest of today. If there are any other meetings scheduled in here, move them." He presses the button on the intercom, not waiting for a reply.

Maria is his lovely secretary, who has to be in her sixties at least. She doesn't deserve to be yelled at—the poor lady. How Theo manages to keep any staff with the way he acts is beyond me. I may have visited briefly during our previous lunches, but spending the entire day with him is a different story. His employees definitely respect him out of fear and not because of his manners.

"You know, I can leave if you need to have meetings in here. I don't mind." I stand and walk over to the little kitchenette area and boil the kettle.

"You're not leaving. Trust me, I want you in here more than I want anyone else who may have been scheduled."

"Okay." I place a tea bag in a cup and wait for the water to boil.

"You're making tea? You don't drink tea," he

comments, without looking away from his computer screen.

"It's for Maria. You could try talking to her a little nicer, you know. It's not her fault you changed your plans today." The kettle whistles and I pour the water in, followed by milk. I grab a muffin off the counter and place it on the tray.

"The paycheck I pay her is plenty nice enough. You shouldn't be making my staff tea, Holly. That's what I pay them to do."

"Well, I *am* making her tea, and I'm taking her this muffin too." Theo stares at me with a look I can't decipher painted across his face. "What?" I ask.

"Nothing. It's just different." He shrugs.

"What's different?"

"Having someone tell me no, or totally disregarding what I've said and doing what they want anyway. No one ever really does that. Well, no one who's lived to tell the story anyway."

"You know, sometimes I forget you're meant to be this big bad boss, then you go and say shit like that, and I remember. Should I fear for my own safety? Worry that I'll end up at the bottom of the East River wearing cement shoes, if I don't do as you say?"

Theo stands and walks over, caging me in against the cupboards. "I'd never hurt a hair on this pretty little head of yours, Holly. Ever. I don't want you to ever be afraid of me." He leans in and kisses my forehead.

Forehead kisses are like my kryptonite. I just melt

into a puddle at his feet whenever he does that. "Good, then expect to be hearing the word *no* for the rest of your life."

"I look forward to it." He laughs as he returns to his desk and sits down.

I carry the tray with the tea and muffin out to Maria. "Hi, Maria. Here, have a break. I'm sorry Theo's so short today. He's dealing with a lot."

"Oh, sweetheart, you don't need to apologize for him. I'm used to it. What's all this?" she asks, pointing to the tray.

"Tea—and a muffin. For you."

"You made me tea?" She looks around the quiet office space. Following her gaze, I notice a few other women staring at our interaction.

"I did. But if you don't like tea, I can make you coffee or a cold drink?" I'm getting nervous with all the glares directed my way. I guess I didn't think this through very well.

"No, I like tea. Thank you, Miss Reynolds. I... just thank you." She nods her head.

"You're welcome. Again, I'm sorry he was so short with you."

"Miss Reynolds, you're a breath of fresh air. Thank you—*again*."

I walk back into the office. Theo is standing in front of his desk, his hands in his pockets and his legs crossed at the ankles. He's lost his jacket and tie, and folded the sleeves of his white dress shirt up to his elbows. The collar is unbuttoned, showing off that smooth, tanned skin.

This, this is a look I want to permanently stamp in my memory. How is someone so bloody attractive?

"Lock the door, Holly." *Oh no, I know that tone.* That commanding presence that goes straight to my vagina.

"I will, but can you just hold that thought for me. One second." Raising one finger, I rush over to the sofa and pick up my phone before returning to the door and locking it. I lift my phone and focus the camera. "Don't move. I need this photo like a fish needs water," I say, snapping a million pictures of my Italian god.

Theo's lip tilts up at the side; he's withholding a laugh. I've seen him do that a lot. Once I have enough images filling my camera roll, I put my phone in my pocket.

"Are you done?" Theo asks.

"For now. But fair warning: if I walk into a room again, only to see you looking all hot and shit, I'm going to want a photo. And that's going to be a lot of photos, because you always look hot. I might need to invest in some SD cards. I won't have nearly enough storage."

At this, Theo laughs—except I'm not joking. I really do want that many photos of him.

"Okay, I'll try to look less *hot and shit*."

"You couldn't, even if you wanted to." I walk forward and stand in front of him. My mouth waters as

I look him up and down. The things I want to do to this man.

Theo reaches out, places a hand on each side of me, and lifts me off the floor before turning around and sitting me on his desk. My legs have a mind of their own, immediately granting him access between them.

Theo's finger runs along the inside of my right thigh, then under my skirt. "I haven't been able to get something out of my mind since we left the café."

"What's that?" I ask.

"If your panties are really wet or not?"

"Well, maybe you need to do your own inspection," I suggest.

"Don't worry, I fully plan on *inspecting* them." His finger slips under the lace and runs straight up the middle of my slit.

"Mmm, I think I like your kind of inspections."

"It's a job I take pride in doing properly." His finger circles my clit, slowly, torturously.

"What's your conclusion?" I ask.

"I think I need to look into things more thoroughly." He removes his finger and slides my skirt to my waist. He then takes hold of my lace panties and rips. I was expecting him to pull them down my legs, not tear them in half.

He spreads my thighs as wide as they can possibly go. Undoing his pants, he frees his cock, lining it up as he enters me with one hard thrust forward.

"Oh God." My legs wrap around his waist. I hold

him close as I let my body adjust to the intrusion. There's always that slight sting when he first penetrates me, the mixture of pain and pleasure eliciting an immediate thrill.

"I think you should come to work with me more often. I could use regular breaks like this," Theo says as he slowly begins to drive his cock in and out.

"Mmm." I have no words as my head falls back on his desk. I'm sure I'm ruining some important documents as I squirm around on top of them. I just don't care enough to stop.

"Fuck, I love your pussy. It fits me like a fucking glove, Holly. I swear you were made for me."

"I'm sure I was." I laugh—although, the more I think about it, the more I realize he might be right. We do blend together really well, and the sex is bloody fantastic.

"Put your hands above your head and hold on to the edge of the desk."

"Bossy much?" I raise my eyebrows at him, and Theo slaps the underneath of my thigh. The sting makes my whole core quiver. Well, that's different. "Oh, bloody hell."

"Hands, Holly, now!" His dominance makes me wetter; I can feel myself dripping.

Following his instructions, I place my hands above my head. The moment my fingers curl around the edge of the desk, I understand why Theo's told me to hold on. He picks up my hips, positioning them at an angle, and he fucks me. Driving in and out, hard and fast. With each thrust, he hits some place deep within me, and it has me seeing stars.

I'm coming minutes later. My legs clutch his waist.

"Yes, come for me, dolcezza. Make that pussy clench around my cock, milking me. Fuck yes! Just like that. I fucking love to soak my cock in your juices."

"Oh God, Theo!" I scream as I follow up my first orgasm with a second.

"Fuck yes. So. Fucking. Perfect." Theo stills as he empties himself inside me. Ever since that one slip up, he's not bothered with condoms. I guess I haven't either. I know in my head it's not the smartest move, but I love the feeling of nothing but skin between us.

Chapter Twenty-Three

I hate fucking waiting for people. It's not hard to be on time to a meeting. Right now, I'm sitting in an empty office, waiting for John Junior, Lana's brother—AKA the new head of the Mortello family. One thing he and I have in common? Being thrown into our roles years before we expected it. It's also the *only* thing we have in common. I can't fucking stand the guy.

People think I'm crazy, but John Junior—well, his craziness knows no bounds. I give him five years *at most,* before it catches up with him and he meets a bullet between the eyes.

I check my watch again. He's now officially five minutes late. I'll wait another five and then I'm out of here. I don't fucking wait on any motherfucker. If he can't show up on time, that's on him.

I watch the clock tick over, and just as I'm about to get up and walk out, he strolls in. Pausing for him to take a seat, I stare the man down, silently trying to gauge what kind of mood he's in today. "You're late," I say.

"It's New York. Traffic's a bitch." He shrugs. "So, whatcha got for me? What fucking idiot killed my pops?"

"She's been dealt with. One of the kitchen staff, a disgruntled woman. I killed her in your father's kitchen." The lie slips from my tongue with ease. I may hate Lana at the moment, but even I wouldn't subject her to her brother's wrath.

"You couldn't have held them on ice for me?"

"They killed my father too. *I was there.* I had to watch them suffocate to death, foaming at the mouth and shit. I had to hear my mother's screams. *Your* mother's screams. I took action then and there."

"Tell me something. Where was my sister while all of this was going down?"

"Right fucking next to me. Why?"

"No reason. She's been awfully quiet about the whole ordeal."

"Like I said, she watched her father die at her dining table. I suspect she's both grieving and in shock." She's probably also caught up by guilt. I know Lana; she plays a tough game but she's never taken a life before. This has to be messing with her head.

"Yeah, you're probably right. So, what now? Are you expecting push back?" John's referring to my leadership of the family.

I may be next in line for the throne, but anyone can try to make a claim for my seat. They won't fucking win it, but they can always try. "No. You?"

"Not that I'm aware of, unfortunately. I could use a good war." He smirks.

"Right. Well, if that's all, I have other business to attend to."

"One more thing. This engagement with my sister. Are you intending on honoring the deal?"

Fuck. I was hoping to God he didn't fucking mention that—it would have made things a lot fucking easier if he hadn't. "And what exactly do you know about the deal?"

"Not much, just that my pops said it was the only way, and that the marriage would solve all of his problems." He shrugs.

"Yeah, well, that marriage won't be happening. Whatever our fathers were planning, it died with them."

"Why? You got a better offer?"

"I can't marry her, John. I'm already married," I say.

"You're married? Since when? My invite must have gotten lost in the mail."

"We eloped, two days ago. It's new."

"Very. And also convenient, considering how opposed to the union you've been. Our fathers both die, and two days later you marry someone else."

"What are you getting at?" Now I'm pissed off. Yes, I wanted out of that deal, but never in my life would I have killed my own fucking father to achieve it.

"Nothing, just stating facts." John stands, and I stand with him.

"Sure, but tell me, John. You have a lot to gain, now that your pops is out of the picture. Any idea on where a humble kitchen girl would have gotten her hands on the drugs she used?" If this fucker is going to accuse me of shit, I'll throw it right back at him.

"I'm not going to dignify that with an answer." He pivots on his heel, stopping when he gets to the door.

"If any blowback comes from this engagement falling through, I expect that you'll support the Mortello family."

"Naturally." I nod. Following him out the door, I head back to my office. I send Neo a text message on the way, asking him to arrange marriage documents for me and Holly—dated for two days ago.

It takes all of three seconds before my phone is ringing. "What?"

"Why the fuck do you need to falsify marriage documents?" Neo grunts through the phone.

"Because I just told John Junior I can't marry his sister, considering I'm already married. Can you do it or not?"

"I can get it done. The real question is: can you get Holly to actually sign them, or are we forging her signature too?"

"I'm not fucking forging her signature. She'll sign." Even as I say the words, I know getting her to agree to this isn't going to be a piece of cake. I feel like I'm ripping her off, taking away the big, fancy-as-fuck wedding she deserves.

I walk back into my office, noting that the two men I posted at the entrance are gone. Opening the office door, I find it empty and my stomach bottoms out. Where the fuck is she? I left her in here.

"Maria, where the fuck did Holly go?" I yell, even though the old woman only sits two feet away.

"She said she was going out to get lunch, Mr. Valentino."

"When did she leave?"

"About fifteen minutes ago."

I head for the elevator, sending Neo another message to get me the GPS location of Holly's phone. By the time the elevator doors open, he replies, letting me know she's in the lobby of this building.

I have no idea how he tracks people down so quickly, but it's a skill of his I utilize often. My heart settles a little, knowing she's in the lobby. That is, until the doors open on the ground floor, and I see her across the room.

My steps are quick and purposeful as I push my way through the crowd to get to her. I glare at my two guards for standing there and not doing a damn thing to stop this. They will be dealt with. But first...

"John, is there a reason you have my wife backed up against a fucking wall?" I growl as I approach them.

I notice the surprise and fear in Holly's eyes. I fucking hate seeing that fear there. John takes a step back. The three men following me surround us, ready for a fight. I flick my gaze to the other two useless fucks who never should have allowed the bastard to get his dirty fucking hands anywhere near Holly. I narrow my eyes in their direction; they've just realized their mistake. Good, let the fuckers sweat a bit before I fucking cut their throats out.

"Your wife? Funny thing. When I asked sweet Holly here who she was, she didn't introduce herself as your wife." The fucker runs his eyes up and down her body, while visions of gouging those same eyes out invade my mind.

Pushing myself between them, so that Holly is now behind me, I don't miss a beat. I won't let this son of a bitch get the best of me. "She wouldn't have. She's not stupid; we're keeping it quiet. We were waiting until after my father's funeral to make the announcements, but now you've gone and messed up our plans."

"Why wait? If I had a piece of ass as hot as that, I sure as fuck wouldn't be waiting to let the world know I owned it."

I know he's trying to goad me. I get it. But wives and daughters have always been off-limits in our world. No one disrespects the women belonging to a made man. This fucker just showed a huge amount of disrespect to the wife of a Don. *And I can't just let that go.* For both personal and professional reasons.

My arm pulls back, and I land a right hook across the fucker's jaw. I've wanted to do that for a long time. Before I know it, I'm on top of this motherfucker, laying down punch after punch. I hear Holly scream. I look around to see one of my men holding her back and out of the way. While I'm distracted, John gets the upper hand, flipping us over and bloodying his knuckles against my nose and jaw.

Then he aims for my ribs. I block the best I can in this position. I get my hand around his throat and squeeze. The problem is: I know I can't kill him. But I sure as fuck can hurt him. I'm about to turn us back over when I hear the unmistakable click of a safety disengage. We both still and look up. My guys have guns aimed at John's men, while John's men have guns aimed at Holly. Fuck, Holly... who is currently pointing the hot end of a barrel at John's head.

How the fuck did she get that? Why the fuck did I think it was a good idea to get her over her fear of guns?

"Fuck, dolcezza, put the gun down," I tell her in a calm voice.

"Oh, don't worry, I plan to. Right after this asshole gets the fuck off you," she seethes.

"What the fuck are you all waiting for? Shoot the bitch," John yells at his men—all of whom look from him, to me, to Holly. No one knows what to do. They may follow his orders, but there are rules in our world. And his own men aren't ready to break them, even at his behest.

I push John off me. Jumping to my feet, I take the gun out of Holly's hand and tuck her behind me again. "I think you've overstayed your welcome, *my friend*. You should leave." My voice is calm, while my mind and heart are anything but.

"This isn't over, Valentino. Watch your back. And hers." He nods towards Holly.

"Come on, John, even you're not stupid enough to threaten my wife—the wife of a Don."

I can see my words sink in when his face hardens. He knows Holly is untouchable unless he wants to start a war. If he were to even consider it, I'd have the backing of the other three families, while he went in it alone.

All five families are allies, but if someone goes rogue and breaks one of our cardinal rules, that someone would be out on their own. Once I see John

Junior and his men exit the building, I turn around just in time to catch a falling Holly.

"Fuck." Scooping her up in my arms, I walk towards the elevator.

"Get those two to the den, *now*." I gesture to the men previously tasked with protecting Holly. Gabe, who is holding the doors to the elevator, nods his head in silent agreement—he'll get it done.

Chapter Twenty-Four

Confusion settles in. Why am I being carried? Why is Theo carrying me? "Stop. Put me down."

"Not a fucking chance, dolcezza," he grunts and holds me tighter.

"What happened? I'm fine. I can walk." I wiggle in his arms, not that there is any use as he maintains his vise-like grip.

Theo looks down at me for only a moment, but I see it. His eyes are stormy dark—he's mad. Then it all comes back to me... what just happened in the lobby.

But why is *he* mad? I'm the one who was scared to bloody death.

He storms through his office doors, and I'm mortified. Everyone just saw him carrying me in here. I can feel the tears burning in my eyes. I need to get away. I need to be alone so I can just let them fall.

Theo puts me down on the sofa gently, a stark contrast to how he's looking at me right now. I watch as he walks over to his bar and fills a glass with amber liquid, downing it before he spins around and pins that icy glare on me. "What the fuck were you thinking, Holly? Do you have a fucking death wish?" he yells, throwing the now-empty glass at the wall.

I'm stunned. I don't know how to respond to him. He's never raised his voice at me. I've never been afraid of Theo, but right now, he's scaring the shit out of me. Okay, maybe I was afraid the first day I met him as he invited himself into my apartment. But since then, I haven't even *considered* him any sort of threat. Not to me.

Until now... He's never looked more like the mob boss he is than right now. I have a sudden urge to get away.

To escape.

I can't do this.

I can't do confrontation.

I silently rise to my feet and walk over to the bathroom. He watches me like a lion ready to pounce on his prey. Opening the door, I begin to squeeze through but I don't get it shut before he's on me. He pushes his way into the bathroom, backing me up against the counter.

"Stop. Please." My voice comes out as a whisper—a plea. My hand lightly touches his chest. The fact that I'm terrified of him, yet still reaching out as if I want to jump his bones, is confusing the hell out of me. I want to push him away. I want to escape his unnerving proximity, and at the same time, I want his arms to wrap around me and comfort me like only he can.

"Fuck, Holly, I'm not going to fucking hurt you. I would never hurt you." He steps back, giving me a little space. His fingers run through his hair, pulling at the tips. I can see he's trying to rein in his temper, but he can't hide the fact that he's mad as hell. I don't say a word. I just stand there like a deer in headlights, unable to move. "Fuck!" he screams, before charging at me again and slamming his lips down on mine.

His kiss is angry—*passionate*. I can feel every emotion in the gesture. I close my arms around his neck and pull him closer. I need him closer. There's something in his darkness that calls to me, no matter how terrified I am of it. Then, just as quickly as he launched himself at me, he pulls away, swinging around and raising a gun at something... or someone.

"Jesus-fucking-Christ, Neo, you almost got your head blown off." T tucks his gun back into the holster.

"Don't shoot the messenger—*literally*. I can always come back later?" Neo raises his hands in surrender.

"No. Did you get what I asked for?" T snaps at him.

"Yep, sure did. But why anyone would actually sign this shit and be stuck with your cheery ass for the rest of their life is beyond me. Holly, blink twice if you want me to get you out of here." Neo looks past T, to me, with a smirk on his face.

"Fuck off. Give me five minutes," T growls, before turning around and kicking the bathroom door shut. Theo takes my face in his hands, lifting my eyes to meet his. "I'm sorry I yelled at you. I shouldn't have lost my temper. Not in front of you." I don't know what to say, so I say nothing. I just stare into the dark depths of his eyes and hope to God I'm not wrong about him. That he is good, no matter how much *bad* he's done. "Dolcezza, you are everything to me. I don't know what I'd do without you. What you did downstairs..." He takes a deep breath, almost like he's trying really bloody hard to maintain his composure. "It was care-less. You're not from this life, so I'm sure you don't understand the repercussions associated with holding a gun to a Don's head. Why the fuck would you do that?"

"I-I was scared he was going to hurt you," I tell him.

Theo smiles—a real smile—the kind that reaches his eyes. "I can handle myself. He wouldn't have killed me. There are rules, and killing another Don is a big fucking no-go."

"You're burying your father on the weekend, T. Someone obviously didn't care much for your rules."

"You're right. But that was different," he says, not making eye contact.

"Theo, who killed your father?" I've had my suspicions, but I'd never voice them.

"I can't tell you that, Holly. You can't ask me questions like that. I don't ever want to lie to you, but that? I can't tell you that."

"Was it Lana?" I probe and watch as his eyes twitch.

"What makes you think it was Lana?"

"Just a hunch. I'm the quiet observer. I'm usually good at reading people. And with the way you flinch every time someone mentions her name..." I shrug. "I just figured something had to have happened."

"You need to keep these observations to yourself, Holly. Do not ever talk to anyone other than me. *About anything*. Understand?'

"Okay."

"I need you to promise me something," he says.

"What?"

"Promise that no matter what happens, you won't

leave. Promise that no matter how much you may not like or agree with my decisions, you'll remember that I fucking love you more than anything else in this world. Everything I do is to protect you. Promise you won't forget that."

"Okay, I promise." I've noticed he asks this a lot of me, especially when he is feeling out of control. These verbal declarations seem to ease his distress, so I will give them as often as he needs to hear them.

"No! Theo, no, I can't do this." All those promises suddenly make sense. "You must have had one too many knocks to the bloody head—you're literally insane. *This is insane.* Neo, tell him it's insane." I pace up and down Theo's office, briefly stopping at the bar to pour myself a shot of tequila, before continuing the repetitive, anxiety-induced movements.

"Sorry, Holly, it has to be done." Neo shrugs.

"Holly, dolcezza, you agreed to marry me just this morning. This is not insane," Theo says calmly.

"I thought I was agreeing to an engagement. *A long engagement.* To planning a wedding that I could have my family here to witness. You want me to just sign a bunch of documents—and poof—we're married as of two days ago?"

"You can still plan your dream wedding; you will still have everything you want. I will make sure your family is there for it. I'll make sure you get to have your father walk you down the aisle. Dolcezza, you can still have all of that. This is just a formality—it means you're mine. It makes you family. It makes you the fucking queen. It makes you untouchable."

"My father?" I laugh. "Really, have you listened to anything I've said? Ever? My father's in prison for at least another ten years. Are you suggesting we wait a decade for this *dream wedding?*" I counter, using finger quotes to stress my point.

"We won't be waiting a decade. Your father will be out by the end of the month, Holly." Theo speaks as if it's fact.

What? He doesn't know what he's talking about. There is no way my father's getting out early. *This early.*

I shake my head no. "I don't know what kind of sick game you're trying to play, but that's not funny, Theo." I pack my laptop in my bag, collect my phone from the table, and glance back at Neo and Theo, who are looking at me like I'm a deranged cat—held above the bath water—but not yet ready to dive in. Speaking of... "I'm going home. I need a shower and to get some sleep." I turn on my heel and start towards the door. Theo is two steps ahead of me. He's always bloody two steps ahead of me. He pauses in front of the door, blocking my exit. "Move," I say more fiercely than even *I* thought I was capable.

"No. I can't let you walk out of here, Holly. Not by yourself, and not before you sign those papers."

I laugh. If he thinks he can intimidate me into a marriage contract—well, actually, he probably could. But that doesn't mean I have to make it easy for him. I storm over and plop myself on the couch, folding my arms over my chest. I raise my eyebrow at him. Theo comes and squats in front of me. He's either stupid or really bloody brave. Because, with the way he's squatting, my foot has a direct path to his balls. It's itching to kick up and give him what for, but then I remember I might actually want babies with this asshole someday.

My mind is all over the bloody place. I should call Reilly—she'll calm me down. She always knows what to do. Usually... The only thing is: I can't tell her that I've gone and fallen in love with an asshole mob boss, who is insisting on marrying me and making me his queen.

"Holly, I'm sorry. I am fucking sorry it has to be this way. Believe me when I say that I want you to have the world. I want you to have everything you've ever dreamed of. *And more.* But most of all, I want you fucking safe. I need you safe."

Well, he started off good. "I'm not safe though, am I? I was just approached in the lobby of *your* building by what looks to be one of *your enemies*, all while *your* men—who were meant to be following me for *my protection*—stood there and did nothing."

"And they will be dealt with. I swear to you: they won't get the opportunity to make that mistake again."

"Why do we have to be married? Why the rush?" I ask. I'm trying to understand his urgency. I really am.

"I may have lied and told Lana's brother—the new head of her family—that we eloped two days ago. He was pushing that bullshit union again, and at the time, it was the only way I could think to shut it down. And then you went and made things worse by holding a gun to his head. He's not going to forget that, Holly. He will want revenge, and if he finds out we're not married… well, you're not protected, and he can do whatever he wants without consequence. This way, I have the backing of the other families. You're guaranteed their protection as well as my own."

I pull out my phone. I may not be able to tell Reilly everything, but I need to hear her voice. I need clarity, and my sister gives me that.

"What are you doing?"

"Calling my sister, or is that not allowed?" I ask sarcastically.

"You're allowed to do whatever you want, Holly."

"As long as I don't leave, right?" The moment the words are out of my mouth, I know I've hurt him. It was the first thing he made me promise, and I intend to stick to that promise. Despite this situation he's gotten us into…

Us. I've never really been part of an *us* before. I really like it. Damn him.

I dial Reilly's number and wait for her to answer. "Holly! Oh. My. God! I was just about to call you. Have you heard?" she squeals through the receiver.

"Heard what?" I ask.

"Dad's getting an early release, something about how his lawyer found a flaw in the paperwork or something. I don't understand it, but I don't care. Dad's getting out next week."

"What?" I look up to Theo, who is wearing his poker face. He knew this was going to happen. I didn't believe him. Did he do this? That's crazy... How could he have done this?

"Dad's getting released. Look, I know you start your new job next week, but you'll come home over Christmas break, right? You have to come home."

"Um, Rye, I gotta go. I'll call you back. I'll see what I can do about Christmas." I hang up before she can say anything else. "I-I need to go to the bathroom." I try to hold back the tears. It's hard.

"Neo, I'll call you later," Theo says, without dropping his eyes from mine.

"Sure, boss." Neo pauses in front of me before he exits the room, the click of the door echoing in the silence.

"I-I need to go to the bathroom," I say again.

"No, you don't. You don't need to hide from me,

Holly. Not ever." Theo picks me up and places me on his lap so I'm straddling him.

I can't stop it anymore; the tears fall down my face. I'm crying in front of him. I don't cry in front of people. I bury my head into his chest and let him comfort me, as his hands run up and down my back.

Chapter Twenty-Five

Holding a sobbing Holly in my arms breaks my otherwise-dead heart. Every fiber of my being lives for this woman. In the short time I've known her, she's become my everything. I don't know the right words. I'm fucking up royally today. And I need to fucking fix it.

I need to get us back to the good... to the happy place we were in this morning. "Holly, dolcezza, talk to me. What's wrong? Tell me how to fix it for you."

"I-I... my dad's getting out, Theo. He's getting an early release." She picks up her head and looks at me. "Did you do this? Did you have something to do with this?" she asks.

"I thought this was what you wanted, dolcezza. I thought you'd be happy," I say, confused. Is she not happy about this?

"I am happy, but, Theo, he killed a man. Went to his house and shot him, without even blinking. How is he getting released?"

"Holly, he shot the man who killed his son. He served justice, where the system failed. Your father is not a bad person for loving his children."

"I guess. But he killed someone for Dylan... What do you think he's going to do to you when he finds out we're married?" She smiles.

"Well, I think I can handle whatever he brings at me. Besides, your family will love me. What's not to love?" I joke. "Wait, you said *when he finds out we're married*... Does this mean you'll sign the papers?" I hold my breath. I really do not want to have to forge her signature, but I will if it comes down to it.

"I'll sign the papers, on one condition."

"Name it—*anything*."

"We can't tell my family yet. I don't want my sister

getting on the first flight over here to string you up by your balls."

"Deal. I love you, Holly Valentino."

"I love you, Theo Valentino."

I stand up and walk over to the desk, with my new bride in my arms. I need these papers signed before she changes her mind and realizes she can do way better than a son of a bitch like me. I sign my name and then pass her the pen. "Your turn."

Her hand shakes as she signs her name. "I can't believe I'm doing this. This is literally the craziest thing I've ever bloody done. But it feels right. You feel right," she says as the ink dries.

"You're mine now. I'm never letting you go, Holly."

"Good, because I don't think I want you to."

I carry Holly across the threshold, while she laughs at my *archaic* gesture—or so she calls it. And I fucking love the sound. I need to hear her laughter more often. "Welcome home, Mrs. Valentino," I say, setting her down on her feet.

"Thank you. Wait, home?" She raises her eyebrows.

"Did you think you wouldn't be moving in with

me? We're married, Holly. Married people tend to live together."

"Well, yeah, I get that... but I've just signed a lease. I can't just get rid of my apartment. I've only been there a bit over a week."

"You can, and you will," I grunt out, frustrated that she's still fighting me on this.

"You know, you giving me demands and expecting me to follow them is not how this marriage is going to work. I'm not the type to roll over and play dead every time you bark." Her arms fold over her chest. And I can't help but smile. She's fucking hot when she gets all feisty. It's not often that she's comfortable enough to speak her mind like this, but I fucking love it when she does. "What the hell are you smiling about?" she asks, stomping her foot—literally stomping her fucking foot.

"I'm sorry... it's just... you're so fucking hot when you get riled up."

"This isn't funny, T. I'm serious."

"I can see that," I say, trying my hardest to hide my smirk. No one else would ever dare speak to me like this, but when Holly mouths off, I can't help but love it.

"Argh, forget it. I'm keeping my apartment. I don't care what you say."

"You can keep your apartment, but you won't be living there. This is your home now, Holly." I wave my hand around the penthouse. Anyone else would be grateful to share this space, you know, instead of an apartment the size of a shoebox.

"Well, what if I don't like *your home*?" she asks.

"*Our* home. Then we can buy another one—whatever you like." I shrug. I don't give a fuck how much I have to spend as long as she's happy.

"Just like that, buy another house? This is New York, Theo. Houses don't come cheap."

"Dolcezza, have I—at any point—implied that I can't afford to take care of things?" I ask, honestly a little insulted that she'd question this.

"*Take care of things?* We're not living in the bloody 1950s, T. I don't need you to take care of things for me—how many times do I have to repeat myself?"

"You may not need me to, but you will let me. I have the means to give you anything you could dream of having, Holly. Don't deny me the pleasure of providing for our family."

"Holy shit, you're serious."

"As a heart attack. Look, I get it: you're not Italian and you're not from this lifestyle. But there are just some things that won't ever change. The man being the head of the household, providing for his family, that's tradition. It's engrained in who we are."

"Mmm, we'll see. I'm not quitting my job. I haven't even started it yet."

"Fine, but you will need security with you."

"You're insane if you think I'm taking your goons into a school full of innocent children."

"And *you're insane* if you think you have a choice."

"Really? You know what? I'm over this day already. I'm going for a shower."

I watch as she storms towards the bedroom, throwing her bag down before kicking her shoes off and flinging them at the wall. Well, fuck, now's probably not the time to tell her how fucking cute she is...

Deciding to let her have some space to cool down on her own, I head into my office and call Neo. "Boss? You're still alive. I was worried there for a minute," he answers.

"Fuck off. I've got the signed papers on my desk. Come get them and make sure they're processed through the appropriate channels. Also, look into the security at Willow Prep. Holly's insisting on keeping her job."

"Why the fuck would she want to keep her job? Does she understand who she married? What she married into?"

"To be honest, I don't think she knows the extent of the Valentino Empire. It's fine. If she wants to teach, she can fucking teach."

"Okay, well, don't get your panties in a fucking twist. I'll look into their security."

"Thank you."

"Hey, boss, can I be there when you break the news to Aunt Gloria that you went and got married without her?" He laughs. Fuck, my mother is going to have a fucking fit.

"Fuck off. I'll tell her after the funeral," I say. I

don't need to put extra stress on my mother. I hang up and go in search of my new bride.

Heading into the bedroom, I find Holly curled up in bed. I go and shower the grime of the day off before climbing in behind her. Reaching out, I tug her towards me. "I'm sorry it had to be this way. We should have had more time to date. I should have had more time to make you fall in love with me," I whisper, kissing her just under her ear.

Holly rolls over and wraps her arms around my neck. "I couldn't be more in love with you if I tried. Do I like the situation? No, not at all. But I realized something while I was in the shower. It's where I do my best thinking." She smiles.

"And what did you realize?" I kiss her forehead. It's like my lips are drawn to her, wanting to land on her skin as often as humanly possible.

"I realized that this is our story, Theo. It doesn't have to be like everyone else's. It doesn't have to follow societal norms or play out as the people around us expect, because *this is our story*. It's about us and what we want to do. It's our happily ever after, and we get to set the pace of our own narrative, no one else. Just us."

Well, fuck, I knew Holly was smart, but this has to be the best fucking thing I've ever heard. "I fucking love you, and I love our story. I promise I will always strive to give you the happily ever after you deserve."

"You already gave me that, Theo." She pauses. "Okay, there may have been a moment when I wanted to kick you in the balls today, but it was short-lived. I love you."

"I scared you today. I never want you to be afraid of me, Holly." I kiss her lips gently.

"Well, you should work on your temper then. I don't do confrontation well, Theo. I never have."

"I think you do better than you think. Holly, you held a gun to a mafia Don's head today without even flinching." At the time, I was enraged… and terrified *for* her. But, now that I think about it, I couldn't be prouder.

"I only did that because I thought something bad would happen to you. It's different when I see someone hurting you. I want to do anything I can to stop it. It's second nature."

"And I love that about you. But you can't go around shooting everyone *or* threatening to. I'm a big boy, Holly. I've been at this game a long time. I can handle myself. I don't want you worrying about me."

"Well, I think as your wife, it's inevitable that I'm going to worry."

"Say it again," I urge her. I need to hear her say it.

"Say what?"

"That you're my wife."

"I'm your wife." She laughs.

"Fuck me, hearing you say that makes me fucking hard. I think it's about time we consummated this marriage of ours, don't you?"

"Technically, we were married two days ago, and

we've *consummated* plenty of times in the last forty-eight hours, so..." Her words trail off as I make my descent, down the length of her body and to the nirvana I find between her legs. "Ah, sure, maybe we should consummate again—just to, you know, make sure we've done it right and all. Oh, bloody hell, T, don't stop."

Holly's hands tangle in my hair as my tongue swirls around her nub. "Fuck, you're the sweetest thing I've ever had. I'm never going to get enough of you."

My tongue dives into her opening, thrusting in and out. Holly pushes her pussy harder into my face. I fucking love how she becomes so overtaken with pleasure she loses all of her inhibitions. Fuck, I need more. Rolling onto my back, I lift and place her thighs over my head. "Ah, what are you doing?" she asks, confused.

"You're going to ride my face, dolcezza. Grab the headboard," I say, lowering her pussy onto my mouth.

"Oh, shit, don't stop. Bloody hell, God!" Her screams get louder, her hips start to move faster, and she presses down harder. If suffocation is how I'm destined to go out, there is no better way than this.

I can feel her juices running down my chin—*I want it all.* I reach behind her, my finger finding her ass and slowly working its way in. And the moment it does, her body tenses up.

Her thighs tighten around my head, and she shivers through her orgasm. *Beautiful.* She's always beautiful. But this is my favorite look of hers: her head thrown back, her long red hair falling down the curve of her spine, her mouth open in that O-shape, a look of pure contentment in her eyes.

Yes, this is the look I want to see as often as possible.

Chapter Twenty-Six

Holly

I'm nervous. I can't be nervous right now, but the butterflies rolling around in my stomach haven't read the memo. I know T has been putting on his usual mask of indifference, like nothing affects him. This has to be hurting him though. Today is his father's funeral. We're standing on the steps of the church, greeting guests as they arrive, with his mother on one side of him and me on the other.

Gloria was none too pleased to find me here next to her son. Other than an icy glare, which speaks volumes all its own, she hasn't said a word to me. Theo's grip on my hand tightens every now and then. It's the only sign he gives that he's not okay.

I feel useless. I should be comforting him, making things easier. I just don't know how. I'm way out of my element here. I remember the grief I felt at Dylan's funeral—there was nothing anyone said (or could say) that made a difference.

So, I don't say anything. I stand here next to Theo, holding his hand and smiling at people as they greet him and then me.

One man went in for a hug. After Theo growled— yes, literally growled and pulled me out of the man's reach—no one else has tried to do the same. However, they do hug Theo's mother and then him.

There are more people here than I could have imagined. Theo's father must have been well known, and judging by all the tears and distraught expressions, he must have also been well liked—or so one could assume.

I feel Theo's body stiffen as three older men approach the steps. "Gloria, our condolences to you and your family," the first says, reaching out and kissing her on each cheek. Gloria bursts into another fit of tears. "T, we'll talk later." The same man nods at Theo, before shaking his hand and repeating the gesture.

There's a lot of kissing of cheeks. I'm glad Theo

made it known I wasn't one to touch. I couldn't handle all these strangers touching me.

When the first man finally looks to me, Theo offers an introduction. "Hal, my wife—Holly." The initial shock over my title disappears as quickly as it came.

"Holly, what a beautiful name for a beautiful girl. I'm sorry for your family's loss." He leans in and kisses my cheeks—one, then the other. Theo's hand tightens around mine, but he doesn't pull me back.

This exchange is repeated with the next two men as well. I'm introduced as Theo's wife, and they offer their regards before moving into the church. Theo leans in and whispers, "Those are the heads of the other three families. Don't go pointing any guns at them, dolcezza." He smirks as he pulls his face away from mine.

"Funny," I murmur.

The next person to come up the stairs is also the last person I expected to see: Lana, escorted by her brother. She wraps her arms around Theo, and I feel my spine straighten. How she has the nerve to touch him, to offer him comfort right now, I have no idea. My fingers itch to scratch her pretty little eyes out. *She did this.* "I'm so sorry for your loss," she says to Theo.

"I bet you are," I say under my breath, not quietly enough however. Theo pulls me against his side, wrapping his arm around my waist. I'm not sure if he's trying to lean on me for support, or anchor me to him so I don't do anything rash. Probably the latter. *Definitely the latter.*

"Thank you. As am I, for yours," Theo says. Lana's father's funeral has been scheduled for next weekend. They didn't want two on the same day.

Lana walks into the church, tugging her creepy brother behind her. That ass just stood there and stared at us, didn't say a word. So bloody rude. I'm not sorry I held a gun to his head. *But I am sorry I didn't pull the trigger.* The bloodthirsty thought shocks me. I'm not a violent person. Not usually, but something in that man makes me want to hurt him. To see him bleed. What the hell is going on with me?

"It's time," Father Thomas says, propping open the doors.

Theo walks in exactly how we had been standing: me on one side and his mother on the other. We're trailed by at least six men—big men in black suits. It's funny that a funeral is the only place these men actually fit in. They're dressed for the occasion.

The service goes by in a blur. I keep looking to Theo; however, his facial features are set in stone. If it wasn't for the slight tremor to his hand, no one would suspect that he's burying his father right now.

"Theo, would you like to say a few words?" Father Thomas calls out.

For a long moment, Theo sits there. Not moving. Not even flinching. And then he stands, except he forgot the part where he was meant to let go of my hand. He drags me up to the podium, where I position myself slightly behind him and to the left, holding on to that same hand while he addresses everyone. "Thank you, Father Thomas. As many of you know, my father was a great man. A man of honor. A man who put the needs of the family above his own. He was loyal to a fault. My father taught me everything I know. I can only hope to be half the leader he was. But I'll go on, trying to live up to his example."

The crowd stands in silence as Theo leads me back down the steps. He doesn't return to the pew though. Dragging me through a set of curtains, he opens a wooden door. But before shutting it, he stops the two men trailing behind. "Make sure nobody gets back here."

"Yes, boss." Their mirrored replies are cut off by the slam of the door.

The next thing I know, Theo has me in the air and sitting on a wooden bench. His mouth fuses with mine, his tongue pushing in. Rushed. Seeking. I wrap my arms around his neck and pull him tighter against me. My skirt's bunched up, and Theo fumbles to undo his belt and pants, before he pushes my panties to the side and slams into me. Hard.

"Oh, fuck," I cry out, the sting taking a bit to settle. But Theo doesn't stop; he just keeps thrusting forward. His movements are frantic. I've never seen him so desperate. I wrap my legs around his waist and encourage him to take from me. To take whatever it is he needs. If this is the only comfort I can offer him, then I'll gladly give it.

It's not long before my wetness coats our bodies. He slides in and out, and with each frenzied penetration, I think he can't possibly reach any further into my depths. But, somehow, he does. And when he does, it's as if he's claiming a new part of me.

"Fuck, Holly, I need you. I fucking need to feel you come. This, you. You're fucking perfection in my otherwise fucked-up world. Come for me, Holly. Now," Theo grunts.

He reaches a hand between our bodies and pinches my clit. With that one pinch, I'm gone. Soaring over the edge. Stars—*the lot.*

Theo stiffens as his thrusts grow more rigid. He empties himself inside me, before his head falls to my chest. Neither of us move for a good minute. Then I feel it. The heavy rise and fall of his chest, the dampness soaking into my top.

"Shh, it's okay. It's going to be okay. We will get through this together, Theo." My words of comfort are shit, even I know that. My hands go to his hair and lift his head so his eyes meet mine. "It's going to be okay," I repeat. I don't know the grief of losing a parent—not in that way—but I *do* know grief. And while it may never go away, it will get easier to live with.

"He wasn't supposed to go this soon."

"I know, but you have to do this, T. You are a leader. You and I, we're going to do this together."

"I don't know what angel sent you to me, but thank God they did. I couldn't get through this day without you, Holly."

"Well, it's a good thing you don't have to," I say, wiping the tears staining his cheeks. I look around the room, and then it dawns on me: *we're still in the bloody church.* "Ah, Theo, I'm not Catholic or anything, but even I know doing what we just did in church is probably a big no-no, right?"

"It's not like we did it on the altar, babe. This room is just the sacristy." Theo shrugs.

"That sounds like something important, Theo."

"It's where the priest gets ready for the service. Don't worry about it. Trust me, Jesus is forgiving and all. Plus, you're my wife; we haven't sinned. This time." He winks.

Chapter Twenty-Seven

"It's about fucking time you answered your goddamn phone," I yell as soon as I hear the call connect.

"Morning. What's got you all bright and cheery this early on a Monday?" Neo finally answers his phone, after letting it ring out three times. I almost got in the car and drove over to his place.

"Where've you been?"

"Asleep. You do realize it's like six? In the fucking morning."

"I know. Get up and get strapped—we've got a meeting at nine with the three," I say.

The three is how my father and John Senior used to refer to the other three families in New York. We're all supposed to work together, however, my father and John were closer than any of the others. And now I'm wondering what kind of fucked-up shit Mortello dragged my pops into.

"Nine? Why on God's earth are you even up? That's still three hours away, T."

"I'm driving Holly to work in about thirty. I've got shit to do—heading the family is no fucking joke, Neo. The amount of shit stacked up on my to-do list is never-fucking-ending."

"Back up. Holly's going to work? She's really going to keep working after marrying you? I thought that was all just a power play on her end, you know, to ruffle your feathers."

"Apparently not. She's adamant about going in," I grunt. I don't see why she has to go to work. I make more than enough money for both of us.

"I don't like it. That school's fucked up. The things I saw in the teachers' lounge when I hacked into their cameras... Man, it puts a whole new spin on the phrase: teacher's pet."

"What the fuck are you talking about?"

"They were doing it in the teachers' lounge, T. Teachers were doing it, porn-style."

"Fuck off. That's one of New York's most elite schools. They wouldn't tolerate it."

"Well, I saw what I saw."

"Whatever. Be ready by eight. I'll swing by and pick you up." I hang up the phone as Holly walks into my office. I take it back. I take everything I said about her working fucking back. She's wearing a tight black pencil skirt, a white blouse, and a pink cardigan. But holy fucking shit, she's never looked hotter. Her hair is tied back in a ponytail—a ponytail I want to wrap around my hand.

My eyes travel up and down her body, slowly, memorizing every breathtaking inch.

"T, are you having a stroke? What's wrong with you?" Holly waves her hands in front of my face.

"Fuck, dolcezza. This is what you wear to work? I suddenly have the urge to enroll myself in your class."

"That might be a bit hard, considering you're not a third-grader." She laughs.

"Are you sure you have to go to work? You could stay here, bend over this desk, and teach *me* a whole lot of new things. We could learn together."

"Mmm, tempting but no."

"Fuck. Wait. How many male teachers are at this school?" I just realized I'm not the only one who's going to see her looking like this. "Oh, for fuck's sake, there're also dads."

"Huh?"

"Every man in a ten-mile radius is going to notice you, and I won't be there to tell them to fuck off."

"Well, it's a good thing I have this flashy rock to show them. I don't know how I would have batted them all off without it." Holly holds up her left hand, where a sparkling, new, three-carat diamond sits. I gave it to her after we got home from the funeral on Saturday. She follows up her retort with a roll of her eyes.

I don't understand how she doesn't see her own beauty. She's fucking gorgeous. "It's a good look on you, that ring. Make sure you keep it on."

"You couldn't pry it off me if you tried. You, Mr. Valentino, are stuck with me now. There are no returns." Her arms wrap around me.

My hands are quick to land on her ass—her perfect, heart-shaped ass—that's currently hugged by that tight fucking skirt.

"Obviously I'm the one winning when it comes to this marriage. You, dolcezza, are clearly way out of my league. But I've got you now; it's in writing and all."

"Trust me, I'm the lucky one. You are everything to me, Theo. Don't ever forget that."

Her lips land on mine, and I greedily take everything she's offering. After a minute, I pull back. "Sorry, dolcezza, if we want to stop for breakfast before you have to be at school, we should probably go now. Although, I'm more than open to having *you* for breakfast. Right here, on this table." I slap a hand on my desk.

"Again, tempting. But I need Helena's coffee. Are you ready to go?"

"Yep, you got everything you need?" I ask.

"Yes."

"You got that mace in your bag? The taser? The knife?"

"All of those things are in the bedroom. I can't take them into an elementary school, T. There are children there."

"Holly, people take worse than that into those schools. You need to be protected. Don't be fooled by the prestigious buildings and state-of-the-art bullshit— school shootings can and do happen everywhere." I know I'm an asshole for putting these thoughts in her head on her first day, but it's a reality in our country. She's from Australia, where those things just don't happen.

And now she's also married into the mafia, where threats loom in every corner. I need her to be aware of her surroundings. It's unreasonable for me to expect to always be there to protect her. And I know I can't glue myself to her side, but fuck, I really fucking want to.

"Okay, and on that note, I'm going for breakfast. You're either coming with me, or you're not."

Holly goes to walk away. I grab her wrist and pull her back into me. "I'd follow you anywhere, dolcezza.

Don't ever forget that." I throw her words right back at her.

"You know you're meant to be this big scary mob boss, right? But really, deep down, you're just a squishy love-muffin, aren't you?"

I screw up my face in disgust. "Do not ever repeat those words to anyone. Make no mistake: I'm every bit the scary *mob boss* people will warn you about. But for you, I'll happily be your... *love-muffin.* Does that mean you want to wrap your lips around me?"

"I absolutely do. But I need coffee more right now, so let's go."

I follow her out the door. I think I'm going to love our life together. This—waking up with her, getting ready each morning next to her—it's the very definition of marital bliss.

Every good feeling I had this morning has gone out the fucking window. I've only been here for fifteen minutes, and these assholes have already managed to piss me off. "There's no fucking way my pops was gunning for more territory. I would have known," I growl.

They're accusing my father and John Senior of

colluding to take over half of New York, by running the other families off.

"Are you sure about that, T? That whole marriage between the families, that was to build an alliance. We received evidence that John was involved with child sex trafficking. We voted to move in. Your father was the only one who vetoed the decision."

I don't believe it. "My father was many things, but even he'd never get involved in the skin trade—not with kids."

"You're right. He wouldn't. *Knowingly*. Unfortunately, he was blind to everything John was doing. Refused to believe it," Beno says, the head of the Garzo family.

"Where's this evidence? And if John Senior was involved, what's happening now that he's out of the picture?"

"Here." A manilla folder gets thrown at me. There are a few things the mafia won't stand for: sex trafficking, and anything having to do with kids. That shit makes me want to fucking throw up the eggs I ate this morning. Opening the folder, I scan the contents— picture after picture of John Senior and Junior at the docks... with steel cages of children being loaded onto ships. I slam the folder shut and slide it back across the table. I don't need to see anymore. "Look, we know you weren't aware of this. Whether your father knew, and was in on it, is irrelevant now. What we need to do is put a fucking stop to it."

I'd love to put a stop to John Junior. "I'll happily take him out myself if that's what you're after," I offer, leaning back in my chair.

"If it were that easy, he'd already be dead. What we need from you—well, you're not going to like it, but it's the only way we can bring down this whole fucking ring," Beno says.

"Okay, let's hear this grand plan." For the next twenty minutes, I sit and listen quietly, giving each boss the respect they deserve. When they've finished telling me their plan, I agree. It's what's best. There's just one flaw: *I don't want to fucking do it.*

I can't do it. But do I have a choice?

"Are you sure about this?" Neo asks from the passenger's seat.

"There doesn't seem to be any other way. Apart from the bullshit trafficking ring, that asshole is not going to give up his vendetta against Holly. He knows how to get to me, and our codes mean jack shit to him. I have to eradicate him. If this is how I can go about doing that, then I have to do it."

I steal a cigarette off him. I don't want to do this. It's going to break us. I just hope that she'll forgive me. That somehow, we will get through this and come out on the other side. "Just promise me you'll look after her, Neo. I need to know she's going to be okay."

"I would die for her, you know that. But do I think for a minute she'll be okay, mentally? After this? Not a fucking chance, and you know that too."

"I don't have a choice. You know what you have to do."

Chapter Twenty-Eight

Holly

W ow, I've never second-guessed my profession before today. I came in this morning full of energy, excitement, and ideas. It's only lunchtime, and everything I thought I knew about education has gone out the window.

I've never met a more entitled, pretentious bunch of brats in my life. I shouldn't speak about kids that way, but that's exactly what they are: spoiled little brats. With the exception of a set of twins in my class... One boy and one girl, who glare at the other students every time they've refused to do something or threatened me with a lawsuit—or better yet, with their daddies.

It's a little after noon, and I'm hiding in my classroom, trying not to bloody cry. How ridiculous! I can handle this; they're just kids. I'm Holly Reynolds—no, scratch that. I'm Holly Valentino. I can do anything, according to T anyway. I'm still working on believing that.

"Mrs. Valentino?" I look up to find the twins, Gabriel and Gabriella. I have no idea what their parents were thinking with those names.

"Ah, yes?" I'm a little confused, because I've only introduced myself as Miss Reynolds. It was a slip of the tongue this morning, out of habit, and I decided to just run with it.

"We can sort them out for you if you want?" Gabriel says.

"Sort them out?" I question.

"Yep, T would want us to. He wouldn't want anyone disrespecting you. Especially these clowns," Gabriella says. "They just don't know who you are. If they did, they wouldn't be so mouthy."

I'm at a loss for words. "You know T?" I probe. Did my husband seriously put little spies in my classroom? Honestly, I wouldn't put it past him.

"We're cousins—second cousins. But I guess that

makes you our cousin too. Our dad said to make sure we looked out for you today. Nobody is allowed to disrespect the family." Gabriel nods intently.

Jesus, they're actually serious. "Well, I appreciate that. But trust me, I can handle whatever those kids throw at me. I'll be fine. I don't want either of you getting into any trouble because of me. It's lunchtime. You should go and play."

They look at each other before nodding their heads and walking out the door. I know exactly what they just did; they had a conversation without having a conversation. Reilly and I do it all the time. I'm tempted to tell them I have a twin sister too, but I don't. I want to keep Reilly out of this world as much as I possibly can.

After the bell goes, I take a deep breath and prepare myself for the last hour of the day. I watch as my students pile into the classroom in an orderly fashion, unusually quiet too. Huh. Then, they all take their seats and look up at me expectantly.

Gabriella winks at me from her desk at the back. Great. What the hell did those two do? Put the fear of the God (or should I say the mafia?) into these other children. I'm going to have to have words with them about that later. Right now, though, I'm going to do what I came here to do.

Teach.

The afternoon flew by; the students completed every task I gave them without any objections. I'm packing up my things when there's a knock at the door. Turning, I find Neo standing at the threshold with a grim expression on his face. And my heart sinks. "What's wrong? What happened? Where's T?" I ask, looking behind him. Hopeful.

"Nothing's wrong, Hol. T's busy with work. He asked me to be your very efficient Uber driver. I'm here to escort you home." He smirks.

I know he's not telling me everything. I can feel it in my gut. He has a great poker face—I'll give him that —but you can't beat your instincts. And right now, mine are screaming. I need to find T. "Oh, okay. Just give me a few minutes. I just have to run to the bathroom first." I don't wait for him to answer. He does, however, follow me down the hall.

Locking the door behind me, I sink to the floor. Something is wrong. I know it is. I pull my phone out and call Theo. He answers on the third ring. "Dolcezza, Neo should be there to pick you up."

"He is," I confirm.

"Great. How was your day?" he asks, casually.

"T, what's happening? I don't feel good, I feel like

something is wrong. Tell me everything is okay, and that if I let Neo take me home right now, that you'll be coming home tonight too."

"I will always come back to you, Holly. Nothing can keep me away from you. Promise me you'll remember that. I will come back." His voice sounds strained.

"Okay, I promise I'll remember," I concede. Whatever he's doing, I shouldn't be distracting him or holding him up. "I love you, T. I love you so much it hurts when you're not near me."

"Ti voglio bene. Tornerò appena posso. I love you too. Let Neo drive you home." He hangs up the phone before I can ask him to translate. I repeat the words in my head, pronouncing them the best I can, as I open Google translate and spit them back out.

"I love you. I'll be back as soon as I can," I whisper, reading from my screen. Maybe I messed up the Italian. Standing up, I wash my hands and straighten my shoulders. "I'm ready. Sorry." I smile at Neo.

"No worries, bella. This way." Neo holds out his hand and guides me out of the building.

I briefly notice the audience of other teachers staring our way in curiosity. I don't care right now though. Right now, my stomach is churning, this deep-seated dread set firm in my gut.

Half way back to the apartment, Neo answers a call. "Boss?" It's Theo calling him, a sense of relief washes over me.

"I left a package in your trunk. I need you to drop it off to me," T says.

"Ah, sure, let me drop Holly off first," Neo responds, looking to me.

"Hey, dolcezza. I'm sorry but I really need that package. I don't have time to wait, Neo. Holly, do you mind if he takes a detour before taking you home?"

"No, of course not. Whatever you need, T," I agree. I'm actually relieved for the distraction. Maybe if I see Theo with my own eyes, this dread will finally go away.

"Thanks, dolcezza." T hangs up before anything else can be said. I smile—it's been a long day of not seeing or speaking to him. I need him more than I realized.

Ten minutes later, Neo pulls up to the curb of an old house. Why would Theo be here? This is not the kind of place I would have expected him to frequent.

"Wait here. Lock the doors and don't get out for any reason, Holly." Neo jumps out of the car. And I watch in confusion, my heart pounding, as he walks around to the trunk.

Ignoring Neo's instructions, I follow behind him. "Get back in the car, Holly." Neo folds his arms over his chest, standing in front of me while simultaneously blocking my view of the property.

I'm about to tell him where to go, when out of nowhere I'm thrown to the ground. There's a loud noise—an explosion of some kind. The pavement shakes with the force of the impact, and I watch as flames engulf the house. Everything turns to white noise. I push at the weight holding me down. "No, get off me. T!" I yell, or at least I think I do.

My ears are ringing. All I can think is that I need to get in that house. I need to get to T. Somehow Bray's moves flicker through my mind, and I manage to get myself out from underneath Neo. I jump up and run towards fire-engulfed structure when a pair of arms wrap around me.

"No, let me go. I have to get him. T, don't you dare do this to me. Noooo!" I feel myself collapse against the chest behind me.

"Holly, stop, I need to get you out of here."

I shake my head no. I can't... I can't do this. I stare at the house. The house that held my entire world. The same house that's now consumed by flames and ash. I feel my heart break in half, and then everything goes black and my body going limp. I give in to the darkness. I need it to take over.

"T..." It's barely a whisper as the sound parts my lips, and I can feel the pressure of a pair of hands as I'm lifted away from the billowing smoke.

Thank-you from the very bottom of my heart for taking the time to read Devilish King.
The next installment of the Valentino Empire Trilogy is available now.
Unassuming Queen

Holly

This wasn't supposed to happen. This isn't the happily ever after I was promised. He was meant to be here. He was meant to be sitting on this throne. Not me.

I'm not equipped for this. I'm not fit to rule over anything. He says I'm a queen. He even gave me the keys to the castle, but what's a queen without her king? Still a queen apparently.

There's nowhere to hide. There's nowhere to run. This is my kingdom. His kingdom. And I'll do whatever it takes to make sure it's still standing when he returns. Because believing he won't come back isn't an option.

Theo

. . .

She doesn't know it, but I'm watching over her. Assisting where I can. Every fibre of my being wants to storm back through those doors and wrap her in my arms. Yet the one thing stopping me... is her. Because I will put her safety above all else.

They want to believe I'm dead. They want to overrun the castle. Take what my family has gained through generations on that throne. Let them try. Like many before, they'll fail. I may not be by her side, but I have eyes and ears all over the city.

I've left my kingdom in safe hands. They will underestimate her, my little unassuming queen, but that will be their downfall.

She may appear quiet, weak even. But I know her soul better than she does. If anyone can reign in my absence, it's her.

Acknowledgments

Holly's story has been waiting to be told for twelve months. I knew I had to wait for the right time to get her story down on paper, because I knew it would be one for the history books.

Holly and Theo's love is the kind fairy tales are made of. Their story has consumed every part of my day for the last few months, and still continues to do so. I just can't get enough of them.

I wouldn't be here without the help and support of those people who play a very vital role in ensuring these stories make it into your hot little hands.

Natasha, who has been with me since day one back when *Merged With Him* was first released, she has been a godsend. She keeps me organised, reminds me of the million tasks I have to do, and continually acts as my sounding board when I'm dreaming up all the ways I can twist and turn a story!

My beta readers, Amy and Sam, these two are priceless. They both inhaled *Devilish King*, chapter by chapter, demanding more and more each day. They kept me motivated and kept me writing, even on days I didn't want to adult!

My editor, Kat, she's the one who polishes the story to make it the best it can possibly be. I could not do this without her—if I could lock her in my basement and keep her editing for me only, for the rest of her days, I would! Maybe I should ask Theo or Neo to arrange this for me.

I have to thank Michelle Lancaster, the amazingly talented photographer and cover designer, who worked tirelessly on the beautiful covers for the Valentino Series.

Made in the USA
Las Vegas, NV
05 March 2024

86717732R00148